LOVE HAS HIS WAY

The Marquis of Sarne awakes from a drugged sleep to find he has been married.

Caught in a trap set by his bitterest enemy Lord Kirkhampton, he has had supper with a pretty ballet dancer from Covent Garden and is knocked out by his own claret which he sent to her house in Chelsea.

As he leaves the house next morning he finds a woman who looks like a servant girl working in the hall, who tells him she is his wife. Hating her, horrified at what has happened to him, the Marquis tries wildly to find a way to save himself.

How his hatred is not equalled by that of Romana Wardel, how they fight with each other and how Lord Kirkhampton is still seeking to further his revenge, is told in this dramatic and exciting 254th book by Barbara Cartland.

Editor of:
The Common Problems by Ronald Cartland (with a preface by the Rt.
Hon. the Earl of Selborne, P.C.)
Barbara Cartland's Library of Love
Barbara Cartland's Library of Ancient Wisdom

Drama:
Blood Money
French Dressing

Philosophy:
Touch the Stars

Radio Operetta:
The Rose and the Violet (Music by Mark Lubbock)
performed in 1942.

Radio Plays:
The Caged Bird: An episode in the Life of Elizabeth Empress of Austria.
Performed in 1957.

General:
Barbara Cartland's Book of Useless Information.
   (Forward by The Earl Mountbatten of Burma.)
Love and Lovers (Picture Book)

Verse:
Lines on Life and Love

Music:
An Album of Love Songs sung with the Royal Philharmonic Orchestra.

Love Has His Way

Barbara Cartland

CORGI BOOKS
A DIVISION OF TRANSWORLD PUBLISHERS LTD

LOVE HAS HIS WAY
A CORGI BOOK 0 552 11234 8

First publication in Great Britain

PRINTING HISTORY
Corgi edition published 1979

This book is photoset in Times Roman 10/11 pt

Corgi Books are published by Transworld Publishers Ltd.,
Century House, 61–63 Uxbridge Road, Ealing,
London, W5 5SA

Made and printed in the United States of America
by Arcata Graphics
Buffalo, New York

ABOUT THE AUTHOR

Barbara Cartland, the world's most famous romantic novelist, who is also an historian, playwright, lecturer, political speaker and television personality, has now written over 250 books.

She has also had many historical works published and has written four autobiographies as well as the biographies of her mother and that of her brother, Ronald Cartland, who was the first Member of Parliament to be killed in the last war. This book has a preface by Sir Winston Churchill.

She has recently completed a very unusual book called "Barbara Cartland's Book of Useless Information," with a foreward by Admiral of the Fleet, the Earl Mountbatten of Burma. This is being sold for the United World Colleges of which he is President.

She has also sung an Album of Love Songs with the Royal Philharmonic Orchestra.

Barbara Cartland has to date, sold 100 million books over the world. In 1976 she broke the world record by writing twenty-one books, and her own record in 1977 with twenty-four.

In private life Barbara Cartland, who is a Dame of the Order of St. John of Jerusalem, Chairman of the St. John Council in Hertfordshire and Deputy President of the St. John Ambulance Brigade, also fought for better conditions and salaries for Midwives and Nurses. As President of the Royal College of Midwives (Hertfordshire Branch) she has been invested with the first Badge of Office ever given in Great Britain, which was subscribed to by the Midwives themselves. She has also championed the cause for old people, had the law altered regarding gypsies and founded the first Romany Gypsy Camp in the world.

Barbara Cartland is deeply interested in Vitamin Therapy and is President of the British National Association for Health.

AUTHOR'S NOTE

Sophocles (495-406 B.C.) was one of the three great Greek tragic poets. He lived until he was ninety and wrote over a hundred plays for the Athenian theatre. He was a master of dramatic technique and was the first author to write poetry spoken in character. Sophoclean drama is always of living persons choosing their own paths to happiness or disillusion, to success, failure or extinction. In fact, the problems were the same as our own.

The Odes of Pindar were written in honour of the victors in the events of the four huge national athletic meetings of Ancient Greece. He was the greatest lyric poet of the period and was born in 518 B.C.

CHAPTER ONE
1802

The Marquis of Sarne groaned . . . moved slightly and thought that the pain in his head could not be real because it was such an agony. . . .

It seemed a long time later that he opened his eyes, saw an unfamiliar room round him and closed them again. . . .

His head continued to throb. Now slowly, intermittently, snatches of memory came back to him, while there were moments in between when he was oblivious of everything. . . .

He was aware that his mouth was dry, his lips felt as if they were cracked, and he needed a drink so desperately that he forced himself to open his eyes and focus them on the wall opposite him.

There was a fireplace and above it a picture he had never seen in his life before.

There was light coming from an uncurtained window, by which he could see furniture of a quality he would never have had in one of his houses.

He shut his eyes for a moment, then opened them determinedly.

Where was he? And why the devil did he feel so ill?

He moved slowly and as he did so, saw there was a piece of paper lying on his chest.

He tried to look down at it without moving his head unduly and saw that he was wearing his evening-clothes.

What had happened, and why should a piece of paper have been put on him?

It seemed incomprehensible, until suddenly it flashed through his mind that he had been in evening-dress when he had taken Nicole de Prêt out to supper.

Of course he could remember it now—calling for her at the Stage Door at Covent Garden in his carriage and thinking when he collected her from her dressing-room that she looked so alluring that she would want the applause of a crowd.

"Are you sure you would like to have supper at home?" he had asked her as he raised her small hand with its long thin fingers, to his lips.

It was perhaps her hands that had attracted him first, for she used them with so much more grace than the rest of the *corps de ballet*.

"Anywhere that Your Lordship weesh," she replied in her fascinating broken English. "But it will be ready *chez moi*."

It was fashionable for the Bucks of St. James's to pursue the French women who filled many parts on the stage and were on the whole better dancers than the English.

The Marquis had had under his protection a Spanish dancer who had pleased him for over a year, and he had thought that Nicole de Prêt could fill her place admirably which was something he intended to discuss with her over supper this evening.

He placed her wrap consisting of a fur he did not recognise and did not consider a proper frame for her beauty over her shoulders, then they climbed down the iron staircase which would lead them to the Stage-Door.

The Marquis was sure that Nicole would admire his carriage, for no-one in London had one that was smarter or drawn by better-bred horses.

The coachman wearing his distinctive livery and the footmen who opened the door, were receiving admiring glances from the crowd that waited at the Stage-Door to see, not only the principals of the show leave but also to gaze at the gentlemen who escorted them and who had occupied the stage-boxes during the performance.

Nicole de Prêt lay back against the comfortably cushioned inside of the carriage.

"You leeve in great style, Milor'," she said.

"Which is something I hope you will share with me," the

Marquis replied.

By the light of the silver candle-lantern in the carriage he saw her glance at him in an intriguing way from under her long dark mascaraed eye-lashes.

"Ees that an invitation?"

"I will explain it more formally after we have had supper," the Marquis said.

She smiled and he was not certain whether she intended to accept his protection immediately, or whether she would prevaricate a little and make herself 'hard-to-get'.

Either way, the Marquis thought, the end was inevitable.

There was no woman in London who was not ready to throw herself into his arms if he so much as glanced in her direction.

Where the *Beau Monde* was concerned, the Society beauties who were toasted and acclaimed by his friends made it very obvious that he was the man in whom they were really interested.

He had only to enter a room to know that every woman's eyes looked at him invitingly and every pair of red lips was waiting for him to kiss them.

Where the theatrical world was concerned it was easier.

The Marquis had only, as one wag had once said, "to pick the choicest fruit off the barrow."

Nicole de Prêt did not speak, and he liked the way she made no effort to entice him but merely sat waiting for him to talk to her.

He had the feeling that she was a better class than most of the *corps de ballet*, although it was always difficult to estimate the breeding of a foreigner.

"Have you been in England long?" he asked.

"Ever since I was a child."

The Marquis raised his eye-brows and she said:

"My parents came over at the time of ze Revolution. They lose everytheeng they possess. Eet ees why I 'ave to earn my own living."

This was such a familiar story amongst the French women in London that the Marquis did not believe it for a moment.

But because she would obviously expect it, he made a

13

sympathetic sound before he said:

"I can see that the fur of your wrap is not worthy of your beauty. You must allow me to replace it with sable—or would you prefer ermine?"

"Eeet ees something I must consider, Milor'," she said, "but you are veree generous."

"Which is what I wish to be to you," the Marquis replied.

The horses drew up outside a house in Chelsea, and he looked at the place speculatively as he followed Nicole de Prêt from the carriage.

To his surprise when she had accepted his invitation earlier in the day, he had received a note from her suggesting that they should dine at her house rather than in one of the fashionable Restaurants where the Marquis usually engaged a private room.

He had however accepted her hospitality, at the same time suggesting that he should provide the wine they would drink.

He knew from past experience that women of Nicole's class were no judge of wine and he had no intention of ruining his digestion with anything that was inferior.

He therefore sent a carriage during the afternoon to Nicole's house with a case of claret, another of champagne, and several bottles of his best brandy.

"What about food, My Lord?" his secretary, Mr. Barnham, had asked.

He was used to dealing with these things and knew that if the food and wine were not up to the Marquis's standard he would not enjoy the subsequent attractions he would be offered during the evening.

"You had better send a pâté and a round of cold beef in case everything she produces is inedible," the Marquis said.

"If she is French she should know something about food."

"I am hoping so, at the same time, I should like to be prepared," the Marquis answered.

Mr. Barnham knew this meant he must send far more food than the Marquis had suggested, and he hurried away to the Chef with a long list of requirements.

The Marquis however, was pleasantly surprised when he walked into Nicole's house and found it far more attractive than its outside appearance suggested.

Chelsea, where the houses were cheap, was patronised by a number of Bucks when they took a lady under their protection, as it had been since the time of Charles II.

The houses varied considerably and the one the Marquis had in mind in which to install Nicole de Prêt was large and luxurious and, as he had taken the trouble to ascertain, had excellent kitchens.

This was much smaller but tastefully furnished, and the Marquis was not surprised when Nicole de Prêt said:

"I theenk, Milor', we dine upstairs in my Sitting-Room. Eet ees far more cosy than the Dining-Room."

"That would be delightful,' the Marquis agreed.

The evening was moving so inevitably according to plan that he might have been watching a play he had seen dozens of times already.

She went ahead of him up the narrow, but well-carpeted staircase and he admired the lines of her figure and the graceful way in which she moved.

"She is perfection!" he told himself.

He thought with satisfaction that he was going to enjoy his evening and doubtless a great many subsequent evenings like it.

The Sitting-Room which had two windows was well furnished in surprisingly good taste.

There was none of the garishness of brilliantly coloured satin cushions or vulgar souvenirs of the Theatre which cluttered most chorus-girls apartments.

Instead it might have been a room owned by a Lady of Quality, and the Marquis decided once again that Nicole was better-bred than the other girls with whom she danced.

There was a table set in front of one of the windows and on it were four candles which a maid in a frilly apron and a lace-trimmed cap came in to light.

"You sent much food weeth ze wine, Milor'," Nicole said, "which I theenk is an insult."

"I do not wish you to take it as one," the Marquis replied. "I merely wished to save you trouble and

15

expense."

"I 'ave incorporated some of my special dishes with yours," she replied, "and when supper is over, you can tell me which you prefer."

She gave him one of her alluring little glances as she added:

"I shall be veree disappointed if I am ze loser."

"That is something you could never be, not where I am concerned."

She crossed the room to where a bottle of the Marquis's champagne was already open and set in an ice-cooler.

She poured out two glasses and brought one to him to where he stood in front of the mantlepiece watching her, appraising every moment.

Then he took the glass from her and raised it.

"Shall I drink to your beautiful eyes," he asked, "or to our future happiness together?"

"You are very certain that we shall be together."

"That is of course your decision."

He knew really there was no question that she would not accept him, as any woman in the Theatrical world would be only too eager to do.

He had the reputation of being exceedingly generous, as he could afford to be.

The only difficulty, as Nicole had been told already, was that his interest in any woman, whatever her status in life, never lasted very long.

"We might as well face it," he had heard one woman he had dallied with for a short while, say to another, "he is here today and gone tomorrow, so make the most of it while you have the chance."

The Marquis had been amused.

He had known it was undoubtedly the truth. It was the pursuit of a woman which he enjoyed and the hope that as she was new she would be perhaps, a little different from the women he had known previously.

Yet it was too much to hope for any great originality and as one cynic in White's Club had said:

"All cats are grey in the dark!"

At the same time the Marquis liked women simply

16

because they were a relaxation from his other activities.

He was a sportsman who was acclaimed on every race-course, at every Mill, and was the acknowledged champion swordsman of England.

The Prince of Wales asked his advice when he bought horses, and the pugilists he had backed had been so successful that he found it hard with his latest protégé to find him a fight.

Besides his sporting interests the Marquis was continually in demand in the House of Lords.

He was an excellent speaker and when he could be persuaded to take up a cause, he championed it in a manner which made him a favourite with the Prime Minister and hated by the Opposition.

The rest of his time was occupied with his estates.

Sarne, his mansion in Kent, was not only one of the largest and most admired houses in the country, but the parties when he entertained there were so interesting and at the same time, so exclusive, it was said that even the Prince of Wales would beg for an invitation.

The Marquis had other properties, all of which had something interesting and unusual about them, but he expected his houses to excel as he expected all his possessions to be perfection down to the very last detail.

"The trouble with you, Sarne," someone had said to him only last week, "is that you are too good to be true, and the only thing that is lacking as you run over us with your chariot-wheels is that you have not a wife to cut you down to size!"

"Do you really think a wife would do that?" the Marquis asked with a twist of his lips.

"Women have a manner of making any man 'toe the line', in one way or another," his friend answered.

"Then I shall be the exception," the Marquis said. "I assure you I shall choose my wife as carefully as I choose my horses!"

"Knowing your damned luck," his friend said, "she will doubtless be such a high-stepper that she will win the Gold Cup at Ascot and trot home with the Derby Stakes!"

The Marquis had laughed.

"You are setting me such a high standard that I shall be wise and remain as I am—a perennial bachelor."

"You will want a son to inherit so much wealth."

"There is plenty of time for that," the Marquis replied.

He was, as a matter of fact, avoiding marriage because he had seen that as far as many of his friends were concerned, it was a most unenviable state.

He had been fortunate in that he had inherited the title before he was twenty, which meant he had no father to pressure him into an arranged marriage such as was usually accepted as inevitable by the young men of his own age, with whom he had been at Oxford.

"Why the devil did I ever get tied up with that virago who makes my life a hell on earth?" one of his closest friends had asked him two years after they had 'come down'.

"You were too young to know your own mind," the Marquis said.

"*My* mind?" his friend almost shouted, "my father's mind! If you only heard the way he went on at me!"

He mimicked his father's voice as he said:

" 'She will suit you admirably, my boy, comes of good stock and has a dowry of £80,000 which is just what we want at the moment, and there will be more when her father dies'."

"You should have looked at her rather than at what she had in the bank," the Marquis said unsympathetically.

"She seemed all right," his friend said. "It was only when the knot was tied and there was no escape that I realised what had happened to me."

He sounded so unhappy that the Marquis had offered him the only consolation that was available.

"Come and stay with me in Grosvenor Square," he said. "I will introduce you to some of the prettiest 'bits o' muslin' in the whole of London."

"Thank you," his friend said, "and Sybil can scream herself stupid for all I care! If I cannot escape from that strident voice of hers I think I shall go mad!"

This was only one instance out of many the Marquis had of how a marriage could demoralise and upset a man.

While he told himself it was the sort of thing that could

never happen to him, he realised how quickly a woman could bore him and knew that if this was inevitable where his mistresses were concerned, it was no less a foregone conclusion with a wife.

He therefore, enjoyed his bachelorhood and never gave marriage a thought, except when he was reminded by those who could not mind their own business that one day he would have to have an heir.

He agreed that was something he would require eventually, but as he had not yet passed his twenty-ninth birthday there was certainly no urgency.

As he sipped his own excellent champagne the maid brought in a number of dishes which she set on a side-table and the Marquis, who was a connoisseur of food and employed the best Chef in London, walked across the room to inspect them.

They certainly looked and smelt appetising and he thought there would be no need to resort to his pâté which he perceived was also there should he need it.

He sat down at the small table with Nicole opposite him and, as he ate a really excellent meal served quietly and expertly by the maid who was also French, he found himself thinking that once again his exceptional luck had brought him Nicole.

She looked lovely in the candlelight and he liked the way her dark eyes slanted upwards a little at the corners and her face, although it owed a great deal to artifice, was also clear and unblemished.

They talked of the Theatre and she made him laugh with some of her descriptions of the temperaments thrown by the Leading Ladies and the eccentricities of the managers.

"Have you been in the Theatre long?" he asked.

"For three years, Milor'."

"Then why have I not seen you before?"

"Thees ees my first engagement at Covent Garden."

The Marquis was well aware that her salary would not enable her to live in the comfort and luxury of the house in which he was dining, and he wondered if he should ask her who had been her Protector and who in fact, was paying for the very excellent dinner he was eating.

19

As they drank the claret, which was so good that the Marquis had sent a case of it to the Prince of Wales, he was not surprised when Nicole said:

"Ze wine ees delicious, Milor'."

"I am glad you appreciate it," the Marquis said. "I find it exceptional. I had it shipped from France only two months ago."

He saw she was interested, then said:

"It is unusual to find a woman who is discerning about wine. It must be your French blood, or has somebody taught you?"

It was a leading question and he was aware that Nicole evaded it as she replied:

"I am told you have the best of everytheeng at your house, Milor'."

"I think that is true," the Marquis agreed, "but I asked you a question."

"My father taught me a great deal about wines and he also insisted I understand food, French food, of course, which he considered was important."

The Marquis was interested.

"Your father is alive?"

"Yes, Milor'."

"Where does he live?"

"He lives in Little Hamble. You will never have heard of it, but it is a small village in Northumberland."

Nicole spoke as if she had no wish to continue the conversation and it was easy to pause because the maid was clearing away the last of their dishes and setting a silver tray on which there was a coffee-pot beside her.

She filled up the Marquis's glass of claret, having, he noted, opened a new bottle, and put a decanter of brandy in front of him.

All this, the Marquis knew, was preparatory to leaving the room and he felt the meal which had been delicious and the manner in which it had been served, was exactly the right prelude to what lay ahead.

He took up his glass and raised it.

"To a perfect hostess," he said, "and to a supper which I know will be the first of many!"

"You are sure of that, Milor'?"

"Very sure," he answered. "If you are at all doubtful I am ready to convince you that this is a very special evening for both of us."

There was a deep note in his voice which he had always found to be irresistible and as Nicole's eyes met his across the candlelit table, he thought it was a long time since he had found a woman who was so desirable.

He liked the way she made no obvious effort to flirt with him or attract him during supper.

She talked in the same way as a Lady of Quality would have done and she ate daintily with an elegance which would have been perfectly in place at Carlton House.

The Marquis also liked the way she had been evasive about some of his questions.

'There is obviously some secret about her parents,' he thought, 'and even if she has been telling me lies she has been doing it cleverly and so charmingly that I am intrigued rather than sceptical.'

Altogether he thought his new liaison would prove very enjoyable and he pushed the chair a little way from the table and crossed his legs with an air of consequence.

It was not only his possessions that made them run after him as if he was the Pied Piper, it was his excessive good looks, and perhaps the raffish, buccaneering expression in his eyes which told all and sundry that what he wanted he took.

One of the Marquis's ancestors had, in fact, been a pirate, and he remembered how when he was a boy one of his Governesses who was better read than the rest used to say when he was naughty:

"It's no use your behaving like a pirate with me! You'll do as I say or I'll tell your father!"

It had taken him some time to realise that a pirate took by force what he could not get by lawful means, and he often wondered whether if he had not been in the fortunate position of being able to buy anything he wanted, he too would have used force.

If he could not prove it in any other way, he did so by taking the women he wanted, whether they were the wives of jealous husbands or under the protection of a man who could not provide for them as generously as he could.

He had no scruples but although quite a number of men would have liked to call him out and fight for their rights, there was not a swordsman or a pistol-shot who would have attempted to do so, knowing that he was superior in both weapons.

"Tell me about yourself," the Marquis asked now, "I am not so naïve as to believe that there have not been many ardent admirers in your life before me."

Nicole smiled a little mysteriously.

"I cannot really believe Your Lordship wants to hear ze story of my life at this stage in ze evening."

"Why not?" the Marquis enquired. "It seems a good moment. When you have finished your claret I want you to try my very excellent brandy. After that we will find it more comfortable to be closer than we are at this moment."

He picked up his untouched glass of claret.

"You intrigue me and excite me," he said. "And now tell me about yourself."

As he spoke he drank nearly half of the claret in his glass.

Only as it passed down his throat did he think there was something strange about it. Then as he raised the half-empty glass to his nose and smelt it to discover if there was anything wrong, he was aware that something extra-ordinary was happening to his whole body and he was finding it hard to move . . to think. . . .

He struggled against a strange darkness and a paralysis that seemed to be overwhelming him.

Then he remembered no more. . . .

. . . . .

Now it all came back to him and with what was almost a superhuman effort, with his head swimming, the Marquis forced himself to sit up on the bed.

'Dammit, I was drugged!" he muttered.

He could not believe that such a thing could happen to him like any greenhorn who came to London from the country and had his money taken from him by the first prostitute who accosted him in the street.

But now he, the Marquis of Sarne, the man who had

boasted often enough that no-one had got the better of him because he knew every trick in the trade, had been drugged with his own claret by a ballet dancer from Covent Garden!

How could she? Why should she?

Surely Nicole knew what would be the repercussions of such an action on her part?

Any Theatre Manager in London would sack a member of the cast who behaved in such a manner towards anyone as important as the Marquis of Sarne.

He sat up and now with a greater effort he moved his legs off the bed and onto the floor.

As he did so, he put his hand to his forehead almost as if he was afraid his head would burst open or fall off his neck.

'God knows what they gave me!' he thought to himself, 'but it must have been gunpowder for the effect it has!'

After a few seconds he opened his eyes and saw lying on the floor at his feet the paper which had been on his chest and must have been dislodged by his movements.

There were two pieces.

He stared at them for some time, seeing that on one was some writing while the other appeared to be a printed form.

For a moment he was not particularly interested, only concerned with the splitting pain in his head, then perhaps because he was sitting up he began to feel a little more human.

"I must get out of here," he told himself.

There was sunshine coming through the window which was uncurtained, and he supposed he had been there all night.

Finally with once again a hand to his forehead to help steady himself, he reached down with the other and picking up the two pieces of paper, held them in front of his eyes.

On the first, which was written in a strong, bold, hand, were the words:

> *"My first inclination was, having drugged you, to chuck you in the river. Then I thought drowning was too good for you, and have therefore made the punishment fit the crime! Rather neatly, I think!*
> *Kirkhampton."*

23

The Marquis stared at the note, then read it again.

So it was Kirkhampton who had drugged his claret, Kirkhampton whom he disliked and who disliked him, but he would never have credited him with the intelligence to do anything which would humiliate him so effectively.

"Damn him!" the Marquis said aloud, "I will call him out if it is the very last thing I do!"

Then as he looked at the other piece of paper he had picked up from the floor, he stiffened.

For a moment he thought his eyes must be deceiving him and he looked again. It was a Marriage Certificate bearing his name!

He read it and re-read it.

It stated clearly, although he could hardly believe what he was reading, that a marriage had taken place on June 15th—which had been the night before—between 'The Most Noble Vallient Alexander, Marquis of Sarne, bachelor and Romana Wardell, spinster, the ceremony having been conducted by the Rev. Adolphus Fletcher, Chaplain of His Majesty's Prison at Fleet.'

"It cannot be true!" the Marquis exclaimed.

But the Certificate appeared to be in order and he knew with a feeling of horror that the Chaplains who were to be found around the Fleet Prison would perform any ceremony, however disreputable, for money.

Their behaviour was a scandal which the Marquis had heard complained about both inside and outside Parliament for years.

He had not been particularly interested and if there had been a Bill introduced to get rid of such pests he had not been aware of it.

He felt sure now that a marriage-service conducted by a Chaplain of the Fleet Prison was, if he was in Holy Orders, valid. At least he had always heard so.

The Marquis got to his feet.

Perhaps, he thought, this was a joke, a jest played on him by Lord Kirkhampton to pay him back for what he considered the insults which the Marquis had offered him over several years.

The first had been when the Marquis had questioned the

riding of his jockey in a race at Newmarket and after an enquiry the horse had been disqualified.

Kirkhampton had been absolutely furious at the time and told the Marquis in no uncertain terms what he thought of him.

After that they had ignored each other on many social occasions at which they were both present or in White's Club.

Then there had been the time when they had been pursuing the same 'fair charmer'.

She was very beautiful, very flirtatious, with a husband who, although he was distinguished, was very much older than she was.

He was frequently laid up and the lady in question had divided her favours for a few weeks between the Marquis and Lord Kirkhampton and, as was inevitable in such a situation, the Marquis had won.

He had then demanded that she should give up his rival.

"I like you both!" she had protested.

"That is not good enough for me," the Marquis said. "You have to choose, my dear, and if you prefer Kirkhampton I shall understand. I was looking forward of course, to entertaining you at Sarne."

He knew as he spoke he was tipping the odds in his favour.

The Party he was giving at Sarne included the Prince of Wales, and it would be certainly an amusing visit not only for His Royal Highness, since everybody who was really interesting in the *Beau Monde* would be invited to entertain him.

"In the circumstances," the lady had smiled, slipping her hand into the Marquis's, "Lord Kirkhampton will have to dine alone tomorrow night."

It was a victory he had never been in any doubt of winning, but Lord Kirkhampton had naturally been livid with anger.

He tried to discredit the Marquis by abusing him to his friends, but they merely laughed.

"Leave Sarne alone," he had been advised. "Surely there are plenty of other women in the world and other races for you to win?"

Kirkhampton, who was a dark, vindictive, fiery man, had gone about muttering that he would have his revenge.

"I will get even with you one day, Sarne!" he had said only a month ago, when the Marquis had out-bid him at Tattersall's for a horse they both wanted.

"Do you want to bet on it?" the Marquis had questioned mockingly.

He had known as his enemy walked away in a fury that the way in which he spoke had only added fuel to an already hot fire.

Now Kirkhampton had struck back.

It could not be true what the certificate said. Nevertheless the Marquis definitely felt anxious.

Feeling rather unsteady on his feet, he walked across the room and seeing his reflection in a mirror, stopped.

The drug had certainly played havoc with his appearance.

He was unnaturally pale and there were dark lines almost as if they were those of dissipation under his eyes.

His muslin cravat, which had been crisp and spotless last night, clung limply round his neck and his hair, normally arranged in the wind-swept manner favoured by the Prince of Wales was definitely untidy.

The Marquis however turned away from the mirror.

What did it matter what he looked like? All he wanted was to get home and find out what the piece of paper in his hand meant.

He opened the bedroom door and found to his surprise that he was on the second floor.

That meant that somebody, presumably Kirkhampton and his accomplices, had carried him upstairs when he was unconscious.

He gritted his teeth in fury to think he had been so helpless in their hands and wondered if Kirkhampton had really meant to drown him.

He thought it was not an impossibility, for His Lordship was the type of head-strong fool who would do anything to assert himself.

Holding onto the bannisters because he still felt his head

was thick with the drug, the Marquis began to walk slowly down the stairs.

On the first floor the door to the Sitting-Room he had dined in last night, was open.

He could see the table at which he had sat but it was now bare.

The door of the room next door was also open and the Marquis could see it was prettily decorated just as he had imagined Nicole would have it, with the bed draped in pale pink and a flounced dressing-table to match.

The wallpaper and the furniture was all very feminine and in good taste.

It was there that he had expected to enjoy himself last night, and once again the Marquis felt like groaning aloud that he had been made to look such a fool.

He went down the stairs and only as he came down the last flight did he see there was a woman in the Hall.

He wondered if she was a servant, and as he reached the last step of the stairs she rose nervously to her feet.

The Marquis glanced at her, then with a little difficulty tried to pick up his tall hat which he saw lying on a chair opposite her.

He would have walked on towards the door, but the woman said in a small, frightened voice:

"I . . I was told to . . wait for you."

"Wait for me?" the Marquis ejaculated.

"Y . yes."

He turned to look at her.

She wore a dark travelling cape with a plain bonnet of chip-straw which made it difficult to see her face.

"Why are you waiting for me?"

Even as he asked the question he had the horrifying feeling that he knew the answer.

"I . . I am . . your . . wife!"

It was obviously difficult to say the words, but the Marquis heard them.

There was a moment's silence. Then in a surprisingly strong voice considering the way he was feeling, the Marquis said:

"If you are part of this dastardly plot of drugging and

doubtless robbing me, you can tell Lord Kirkhampton to go to the devil where I shall doubtless find him!"

His voice seemed to echo and re-echo around the small Hall. Then as the Marquis turned again to the door the woman said:

"P . please . . Lord Kirkhampton has . . left."

"Doubtless you know where to find him," the Marquis retorted, "and do not forget to give him my message."

He had the door open by now and with a sense of relief saw that his carriage was standing outside.

He had told his coachman last night to wait for two hours, then if he did not have a message from him, to come back first thing in the morning.

It was an inexpressible relief to know that his horses were there.

Seeing him in the doorway the footman jumped down from the box and as the Marquis took another step forward the voice behind him said:

"Please . . My Lord . . please . . I do not know . . what to . . do."

The Marquis paid no attention but moved on towards the carriage.

He had moved onto the pavement when behind him she said:

"If you . . could . . just give me . . some . . m . money . . I . . I could . . go h . home."

"I have no intention of giving you a penny!" he replied and stepped into his carriage.

The footman shut the door and jumped up onto the box.

The carriage drove off and only when they reached the end of the road did the Marquis realise that it was a cul de sac and there was only a crescent of houses at the end with a small garden in the centre round which the carriage could turn.

He therefore was driven back the way he had come and as if he could not help being curious as to what the woman who had spoken to him, had done, he looked out of the window.

He saw, to his surprise a man, doubtless a servant, because he was wearing an apron, putting a trunk out through the door while she stood and watched him.

The man threw the trunk which was only a small one, down the steps, and just as the carriage drew even, he went inside and slammed the door of the house.

As they passed by the Marquis saw the woman sit down on the trunk and put her hands up to her face.

'So she is no more use to them!' he thought with satisfaction. 'That should teach her a lesson she will not forget in a hurry!'

The carriage was held up at the end of the road by the traffic.

As the Marquis leaned back and shut his eyes it suddenly struck him that if the woman he had just left crying on the door-step was really his wife she could, if she told anybody who she was, cause a very unpleasant scandal.

He sighed.

It was not possible! He could not credit it! He would not even acknowledge that she had any right to his name.

But he knew the paper in his pocket had an unpleasant look of authenticity about it, and the Marquis was afraid in a manner he had never been afraid of anything before.

This was a situation he would get out of some way or another, but it might take time and money, and the most important thing as far as he was concerned was that nobody should know that the whole episode had ever occurred.

The Marquis had a quick brain and he realised as they turned into the main street that it would be exceedingly foolish to leave a woman who could make trouble for him, alone in London without any money.

If she was telling the truth, it would only be a question of time before she was picked up by some charlatan who could use her to blackmail him in an extremely unpleasant fashion.

The Marquis made up his mind.

He bent forward to stop the carriage and when the footman jumped down to hear his commands they drove back to the house they had just left.

He half-suspected that the woman who had been thrown into the street had just been another bait to trap him as Nicole had done with her invitation to supper.

29

She was still sitting there, her hands were still over her eyes and she only looked up when the carriage came to a standstill beside her.

Once again the footman came to the carriage door.

"Ask that young woman to join me!" the Marquis said sharply, "and put her trunk up behind."

"Very good, M'Lord."

The footman was too well trained to show any surprise either in his voice or his expression.

The Marquis heard him say:

"His Lordship asks if you'll join him, Ma'am."

The woman obviously hesitated and for a moment the Marquis thought she was going to refuse, then she came to the carriage-door.

"Get in!" he said.

Because he was so angry he could not help speaking in a sharper tone than he would have used to a dog.

She obeyed him, sitting not beside him but opposite on the small seat with her back to the horses.

The Marquis heard the footman strapping her trunk on to the back of the carriage, but he did not speak.

The horses had started off again to drive to the end of the road and turn as they had done before.

Then the woman said pleadingly:

"Please .. may .. I .."

"I have no wish to listen to your lies," the Marquis interrupted harshly. "You will be silent until we arrive where I am taking you."

She bowed her head and he supposed she was crying again.

CHAPTER TWO

The horses stopped and the Marquis stepped out when a footman with powdered hair and wearing his livery opened the door.

He walked quickly up the steps of Sarne House and into the Hall saying over his shoulder as he did so, to the Butler:

"Where is Mr. Barnham?"

"In his office, M'Lord. Shall I fetch him?"

"No. Show that woman in the carriage into the Morning Room."

He walked on over the marble floor without looking back and turning down the corridor opened a door half-way down it.

It was a very comfortable, luxurious office that was in keeping with the magnificence of the rest of the house, and Mr. Barnham was seated at a large flat-topped desk with a pile of papers in front of him.

He looked up perfunctorily as the door opened and seeing who was there, rose to his feet with a look of astonishment on his face.

"What has happened, My Lord?"

The Marquis slammed the door behind him and walked to the desk, throwing down the two pieces of paper he held in his hand and saying as he did so:

"This is what has happened!"

Mr. Barnham picked them up.

As the Marquis had done, he read first the letter from Lord Kirkhampton, then the Marriage Certificate.

"Good God!" he exclaimed.

"I was drugged," the Marquis said, "caught unawares like a nit-wit who has never been to London before!"

Mr. Barnham did not reply. He was still perusing the Marriage Certificate and the Marquis walked across to the window and back before he asked harshly:

"Well—is it valid?"

"I am afraid it may be."

"That is what I thought."

There was such a note of horror in his voice that Mr. Barnham looked up to ask:

"What is she like? The woman, I mean?"

"A prostitute or a servant—I have no idea, but I have brought her here with me."

"Here?"

There was no mistaking Mr. Barnham's astonishment.

"What else could I do?" the Marquis asked savagely. "As the horses turned I saw a servant turn her into the street. It might have been a trick, I do not know. I was nervous in case it was another way of involving me in blackmail, or worse."

"I understand," Mr. Barnham said. "I think it was wise of Your Lordship not to leave her there."

He looked at the Marriage Certificate again and said:

"I have heard of this man Fletcher. There have been representations made about him in Parliament."

"I thought I had heard his name," the Marquis said.

"He is genuinely in Holy Orders."

"Then what you are saying is that I am married—legally married," the Marquis said. "How can you get me out of it?"

It was a cry for help, the cry, his secretary knew, of a man who was desperate.

"We shall have to consider the matter very carefully, My Lord," he said after a moment's pause. "Why do you not bathe and change, have something to eat and drink, while I think about what can be done?"

"I have a terrible feeling," the Marquis replied, "that Kirkhampton's revenge is really effective. That is what you are saying, is it not, Barnham?"

"There must be a way out, but for the moment I cannot imagine what it can be!" Mr. Barnham answered.

"Send for the greatest legal brains in England, make an

appointment with the Attorney-General. If there is a loop-hole in the law we will find it."

"There is one obvious one," Mr. Barnham said quietly. "Divorce."

"And have the whole preposterous situation made public?" the Marquis asked. "Headlines in the newspapers? My friends all laughing at me? I would rather murder the damned woman, and have done with it!"

The Marquis spoke so violently that the whole room seemed to vibrate from his voice and Mr. Barnham answered:

"I imagine that is just what Lord Kirkhampton is hoping you will do."

The Marquis looked at him in a startled fashion.

"You mean that you think Kirkhampton intends to continue this ridiculous vendetta?"

"Knowing Lord Kirkhampton," Mr. Barnham replied, "and being aware of the hatred you have aroused in him and the way he has ranted against you for some time, I imagine that having inveigled you into a trap, he will not easily let you out of it."

The Marquis made a sound of indescribable fury, and clenching his fists he said:

"I would rather kill myself than have him gloating over me."

For a moment he looked so wild that Mr. Barnham was alarmed.

"Sit down, My Lord," he said. "I am going to order you some coffee and some brandy, then we will try to reason this out as sensibly as is possible. I am sure dramatics such as those in which Lord Kirkhampton has indulged will get us nowhere."

The Marquis put his hand up to his forehead.

"All right, Barnham, I suppose you are right. It is only that I feel so damned ill. This, on top of a head which seems likely to split open at any moment, has unbalanced me."

Mr. Barnham thought that in all the years he had been with the Marquis, he had never before known him to admit to a weakness.

For almost the first time since he had been in charge of

the Marquis's domestic life, so to speak, the administration of his estates and his private affairs, he felt very much older and wiser—almost paternal towards the young man whom he had always admired.

As if what he had been saying made sense the Marquis suddenly walked towards the door.

"You are right, Barnham, you always are!" he said. "I will bathe and change. Order me something to drink in here in a quarter-of-an-hour.

He had the door open before Mr. Barnham asked:

"The woman—where is she?"

"In the Morning Room," the Marquis answered. "And let her rot there. I will not even speak to her!"

He did not slam the door as he went out, but the way he closed it made it somehow a more ominous sound than if he had made a noise.

It was half-an-hour later that the Marquis, sitting in front of the breakfast table which was arranged in the office, asked in a serious, almost business-like tone:

"Well, Barnham, have you any helpful suggestions to make?"

.   .   .   .   .

After the Marquis had left him Mr. Barnham had sat at his desk reading over and over again the letter from Lord Kirkhampton, then the Marriage Certificate.

He was even more acutely aware than the Marquis of how bitterly revengeful Lord Kirkhampton had felt at the way in which the younger man had circumvented and defeated him on so many different occasions.

There were always friends of the Marquis who not liking to tell him personally bad news or to warn him about his enemies had found it easier to confide in Mr. Barnham, whom they all liked.

Many of them had at one time or another, been in the same Regiment in which Mr. Barnham had served before a wound on the battlefield had forced him to retire into civilian life.

The Marquis had often thought it had been the luckiest day in his life when someone had told him that Captain Roger Barnham was looking for a post.

"He is well-educated, Vallient, and a thoroughly decent chap," the Marquis's friend had said. "I should think he is just the sort of person who would suit you, if you have a place for him in the running of your vast estates."

It just so happened that the Marquis was thinking of retiring his secretary, who had also acted in the capacity of a Comptroller to his father, but whom he personally found too old and too slow.

Roger Barnham had suited him admirably.

He insisted on dropping his Army rank and had grasped the intricacies of the Marquis's possessions with the same quickness and tact that he soon extended to dealing with his more private and intimate affairs, such as mistresses and lady-friends.

In fact, there were very few secrets that the Marquis kept from Mr. Barnham, and it was true to say that in the years they had been working together they had never had cause for disagreement.

Mr. Barnham was therefore well aware that the Marquis not only had a vacillating heart which was seldom engaged by any woman, however beautiful, for more than a very short time, but also had no intention of marrying, or what was known as 'settling down'.

It certainly suited him for the Marquis to remain a bachelor and have no-one question the way in which he ran Sarne, or any of the other houses which his employer owned, or disrupt the smooth manner in which the servants carried out his orders.

He felt therefore, when confronted by a Marriage Certificate and a woman the Marquis had described as a prostitute or a servant, that it was his problem as well.

His eyes as he looked across the room at the Marquis, were deeply sympathetic, at the same time extremely anxious.

Bathed and changed the Marquis looked his usual elegant self. His cravat crisp and white was tied in the intricate style which was the envy of all the Dandies of St. James's Street and his hair had been brushed precisely back into the windswept style.

There was only a slight pallor beneath the golden tan

which came from being continually out of doors to proclaim that he had perhaps passed an unusually tiring night.

That, Mr. Barnham thought somewhat cynically, was nothing new, except that the repercussions from this one were very different from any indulgences of the past.

The Marquis was waiting for his reply to his question, and after a moment he said:

"I have been remembering what I have heard about this Parson, Fletcher. There was a case about two years ago, I recall, in which his authority to marry a young heiress to some dissolute waster, was challenged by her father."

"And the result?" the Marquis asked.

"The Court ruled that the marriage was valid."

The Marquis's lips tightened. Then he said in carefully controlled voice:

"That leaves me a married man!"

"I am afraid so, My Lord."

There was silence for a moment, until the Marquis said:

"Then I suppose the only thing I can do is to give the woman some money and tell her to go to the devil!"

"I have thought of that," Mr. Barnham replied, "and I have a feeling that is exactly what Lord Kirkhampton will expect you to do."

The Marquis looked startled.

"What do you mean by that?"

"There is a chance in those circumstances that to revenge himself still further upon you he will parade the woman as your abandoned wife, whip up public and social sympathy for her, and in short create a scandal."

There was silence as both the Marquis and Mr. Barnham were thinking how that situation was exactly what was happening in the case of the Prince of Wales and Princess Caroline of Brunswick, whom he had married in order to pay his debts, but to whom he had taken a violent dislike on their wedding night.

Now there were two factions of Society—those who supported the Prince, and those who supported his estranged wife.

The Marquis, who had heard the jokes and the laughter which had humiliated the Prince and infuriated his friends,

36

knew that he could not bear that to happen to him.

It would be intolerable to know that those who previously had admired him for his sportsmanship were sneering and sniggering at him behind his back and he might even, as the Prince was, be hissed rather than cheered by the crowds on the race-course, or at the Theatre.

Again there was silence before he asked now desperately:

"What can I do?"

"I have not of course seen this woman," Mr. Barnham said slowly, "but if it was humanly possible, I should suggest that you made the best of a bad job."

The Marquis stared at him as if he had taken leave of his senses.

"Am I hearing you aright, Barnham?" he asked. "Are you seriously suggesting that I treat this woman as my wife? Let her sit at the head of my table, wear the Sarne diamonds, introduce her to the *Beau Monde?*"

Mr. Barnham rose from his desk to walk in the same manner that the Marquis had done to the window and back again.

"I have been racking my brains, My Lord," he said, "to think what else you can do. We know Lord Kirkhampton will be watching, trying to trip you up, attempting to force you into the position where you will have to excuse yourself and perhaps look foolish in doing so. Unless she is completely and utterly impossible, there must be something we can make of her."

He threw out his hand.

"If she is uneducated, uncouth and ungraceful she can be tutored into some semblance of acceptability. If she is young enough to be adaptable, nothing is impossible."

The Marquis stared at him in a bemused fashion. Then he said almost beneath his breath:

"Tutored into becoming my wife? My God, Kirkhampton has certainly got the revenge he looked for!"

"It may not be as bad as you think," Mr. Barnham said quickly, as if he wished to reassure himself as much as the Marquis, "if she is an actress like Nicole de Prêt."

"Nicole de Prêt!" the Marquis repeated. "She is at the bottom of all this! How can I have been such a fool, such an abject fool, as not to have found out who her Protector was before I invited her out to supper?"

He knew as he spoke, it was because he was so used to getting exactly what he wanted in life, and sweeping aside everybody else's considerations, knowing there was practically no woman on the stage, or in any other stratum of Society who would not willingly relinquish her present lover, if she had the chance of attracting him.

The Marquis admitted to himself that he had been too puffed up with his own consequence, too sure of his own fascinations.

For the first time, and it actually was the first, he had met a woman who preferred another man to himself, and that man unbelievably was Lord Kirkhampton!

Mr. Barnham broke in on his thoughts.

"I think, My Lord, what we should do now is to go and have a talk with this woman and find out, if we can, who she is, and where exactly she fits in to this extremely unpleasant plot. We shall also know better after we have seen her what will be best to do in the future."

"What would be best," the Marquis said, "is if we could get this marriage declared null and void. You do not think we could bribe Fletcher?"

"That would not only be an impossibility from a legal point of view," Mr. Barnham replied, "but even to approach him might be dangerous. You can be quite certain that Lord Kirkhampton will anticipate that you might try such a thing."

"Kirkhampton!" the Marquis muttered the words between his teeth. "If I had the chance of killing him at this moment, I would not hesitate!"

"I am sure he will be waiting for you to call him out and will make the very most of such an action on your part."

"How?"

"Think if you were in Kirkhampton's shoes," Mr. Barnham said. "At the moment he is holding all the aces. He had the most important, most admired and eligible bachelor in the whole of the *Beau Monde* married

38

ignominiously and without his knowledge being unconscious, to an unknown woman!"

The Marquis groaned, but he did not interrupt and Mr. Barnham went on:

"It is a story which will lose nothing in the telling, as you can be quite sure, and no-one will enjoy telling it more than Kirkhampton. But it is such an incredible, such an unlikely tale where you are concerned, that unless he has some circumstantial evidence to support his contention I very much doubt if anybody will believe him."

The Marquis sat up in his chair.

"Go on, Barnham," he said. "You are beginning to make sense."

"Kirkhampton will hope that you will either try to get the marriage annulled, disprove its validity or, as you have just yourself suggested, call him out for perpetrating such a trick upon you. If you take any of those actions, that will prove conclusively that his very strange tale is true."

"Yes, yes. I see that," the Marquis agreed.

"So we get back to what I suggested in the first place," Mr. Barnham said. "If the woman is at all presentable, if there is anything we can do to make the marriage appear to be quite a genuine action on your part, then Kirkhampton's whole strategy falls to the ground. No-one will believe him and anything he attempts to say will merely sound foolish and spiteful. Everyone knows already that he is your enemy and prepared to disparage you in any way he can."

The Marquis rose.

"You are right, Barnham—of course you are right!" he said. "But everything hinges on one thing."

"What is that?"

"What the woman is like, and the only thing I can suggest we do now is to go and look at her."

"Exactly, My Lord, and after that we shall have a better idea of what our chances are against an evil but, I have to admit, a clever antagonist."

.   .   .   .   .

In the Morning Room, where she had been shown by the Butler after she entered Sarne House, Romana had sat down on the first chair she came to and once again put her hands up to her face.

She had not been crying, as the Marquis had thought, in the carriage. She had only been feeling desperately that this was a nightmare from which she could not awake, could not come back to sanity.

Everything that had happened to her since she came to London made her feel as if she was encompassed by a dark fog through which she could not see and could not find her way.

Now she thought dispairingly that even if she obeyed her impulse to run away, she had no money, and she doubted if she found her way to a Church or some charitable institution, whether they would help her to return home.

Her lips felt dry and she thought it must be fear rather than thirst. But she did not dare ask if she could have a glass of water although she remembered that she had had nothing to eat since tea-time the day before when the stage-coach had stopped on the outskirts of London.

One of the horses had cast a shoe and by the time a blacksmith had been found much time had passed and they had arrived in London far later than she had expected.

She had therefore arrived at the house of her friend, Nicole de Prêt, in Chelsea, several hours later than she had intended, and it was in that moment that everything had begun to happen.

The hackney-carriage had put her down at the door and she spent her last shilling in paying the driver.

When she knocked it had been quite a long time before she heard footsteps from inside the house.

In fact it had been so long that she had thought for one frightening moment that Nicole could not have received her letter, or had gone away.

When the door had been opened, to Romana's surprise, by a man-servant wearing a livery trimmed with silver-crested buttons.

Nicole in writing home to her friend had spoken of the excellent position she had obtained in the Dancing-School; but Romana was aware that the salary of a dancing-mistress, however talented, did not usually extend to the employment of men-servants, or for providing them with a livery.

However the servant was waiting for her to speak and she asked:

"Is Miss de Prêt at home?"

"Is she expecting you?" the man asked, in what Romana thought was a somewhat aggressive fashion.

"Yes, but I am afraid I am rather late," she replied.

The man looked at her uncertainly as if he was not sure what to do.

At that moment a door behind him opened and a gentleman stepped into the Hall.

He wore evening-clothes which had an elegance which Romana had never seen before. There was a flashing diamond in his shirt-front and his fob glistened against his black satin breeches.

"Who are you?" he asked sharply.

Surprised by his tone and his appearance Romana replied:

"Perhaps I have come to the wrong house . . I thought Miss Nicole de Prêt lived here."

"She does! What do you want with her?"

"I wrote to her that I was coming and asked if she would have me to stay for a short while until I could obtain employment in London."

She thought the man looking at her appeared surprised. Then he said:

"Employment? What sort of employment do you expect to get, or is that an unnecessary question?"

"Nicole told me she had a very good . . position in a Dancing-School . . and I can dance, but not as well as she . . and I thought . . perhaps she might introduce. . ."

Before she could say any more the man put back his head and laughed.

"Dancing-School? So that is the tale she tells them at home. Oh, well, never tell the truth if you can lie. That is as good a motto as any other!"

Romana looked at him.

"I do not . . understand."

She thought as she spoke that the gentleman was looking at her in a strange way. Then he said:

"Come in here. I want to talk to you. Nicole is busy at the moment. I expect she will see you later."

He indicated with his hand the room from which he had just emerged. At the same time, he said to the servant who was obviously awaiting instructions:

"Bring in the lady's trunk."

Romana knew there was nothing else she could do and bewildered by this unexpected reception she entered a small Sitting-Room which looked onto the back of the house.

It was well furnished, she thought, and she was reassured that Nicole was really there by recognising several objects that were familiar.

The work basket that Romana's mother had lined for her with cushioned blue satin before she left for London, a water-colour of the River Hamble which she and Nicole had both sketched a dozen times when they had shared a Governess.

It struck her that Nicole must be entertaining and she had arrived at an inopportune moment, so she said apologetically:

"I am sorry that I am so late, but the stage-coach was . . delayed at Potters Bar, or I would have been here . . some hours ago."

"Nicole did not tell me she was expecting you," the gentleman said.

Romana wondered why he should expect her to do so. Then she said in a worried voice:

"Perhaps I should have waited for her reply, but as I explained in my letter, after my father died the Mortgagees found a purchaser for the house and they required immediate possession. I had to leave and I felt sure that Nicole would understand and help me to find employment as she has done."

"You are an orphan?" the gentleman enquired.

Romana had seated herself on a small sofa and the gentleman standing with his back to the fireplace seemed, she thought, overwhelming and still somewhat aggressive.

For some reason or other she did not like him and she thought in fact he was not the sort of friend Nicole, who was sensitive and sympathetic, should have had.

There was something hard about this fashionable figure that made Romana feel insignificant and somehow uncomfortable.

It was perhaps the way he kept looking at her, the way she felt he was appraising her countryfied clothing, and perhaps too, the fact that she was tired and travel-stained after such a long journey.

"Yes . . I am an . . orphan," she agreed in answer to his question. "My mother died two years ago and my father last week. He had not been well for some time."

She tried not to let her voice break as she spoke to him, knowing that here in London she felt even more lonely and lost than she had in Little Hamble when she had discovered that she had not only lost her father but also her home.

It had never struck her for one moment that although they had always been hard up there would be no money left for her when her father died.

His illness had been expensive and she knew too late that she should have taken matters into her own hands and dismissed the servants and sold several of the horses.

She should have cut down in all sorts of different ways long before she was faced with the frightening fact that for the last year they had been living on borrowed money, and the Bank would no longer cash their cheques and there were large amounts outstanding.

"How could I have been so foolish as not to have realised these things before?" she asked.

She knew it was because her father had always taken charge of everything and had not confided in her for the simple reason that while he talked to her as an equal in intellect, he always thought of her as a child.

When she had left the family vault and walked back alone to the Manor House which had been her home all her life and which was already in the possession of the Mortgagees, she had known for the first time in eighteen years she had to stand on her own feet and think for herself.

It was then she had realised there was no way that she could possibly earn money in Little Hamble.

How could she ask a farmer from whom they had always

43

bought their eggs, their butter, their milk and their cream if she could work as a milk-maid?

Or how could she ask the old couple who kept the village shop if they would employ her, when they had half-a-dozen children to do it for nothing?

She had to go away and the only person she knew outside the village who was earning her living, was Nicole.

It was natural that she should turn to a trusted friend with whom she had been brought up; indeed Nicole was almost like a sister.

Romana had gone from the funeral straight to the de Prêts who lived at the other end of the village.

Neither the Comte nor the Comtesse had been well enough to come to her father's funeral, although she had received a letter of sympathy from the Comtesse.

Written in the pure classical French which they always spoke, she told Romana how deeply they felt for her and how their thoughts and their love were with her at this tragic time.

"I thought, *Madame*," Romana said to the Comtesse, "that as I have to earn my own living I would go to London and ask Nicole to help me."

"But, of course, *ma petite*," the Comtesse had said. "Nicole will look after you and help you as she has always been ready to do. After all, she loves you as we do."

"That is what I thought you would say," Romana said, "and I think I ought to leave at once."

She knew as she spoke that it was important that she should do so.

The Mortgagees had told her that the new owner of the Manor wished to move in immediately and she had only two days in which to pack her belongings.

She could not ask to stay with the Comte and Comtesse, for their cottage was so tiny that it contained only two bedrooms.

Since the Comte had been so ill he had a bedroom to himself, while the Comtesse slept in what had been Nicole's room before she left home.

Romana had therefore sent a letter post-haste to Nicole which she knew would arrive some days before the much slower stage-coach could rumble from the North to the South.

She told Nicole of her difficulties and hoped she could help her, knowing that all through their lives they had shared everything together.

Nicole was two years older than she was and had already been in London for eighteen months, writing home excitedly to say what a wonderful position she had found in a Dancing-School.

She sent her father and mother money which had made them proud of their daughter's cleverness. It had also made all the difference to their being able to afford the little luxuries which the Comte's illness had made so necessary.

'I can dance too,' Romana thought, 'not as well as Nicole, but well, and I could easily teach the very young children while Nicole concentrated on the older ones.'

She had a very vague idea of what a Dancing-School entailed, but Nicole had spoken of it in such glowing terms that it was obviously a very superior one.

Romana was certain that it would need new teachers and of course, for a probationary period, she would be prepared to accept a very small wage.

It all seemed, she thought as she journeyed in the slow, often overcrowded stage-coach, a plan that alleviated a great deal of the misery and unhappiness she felt at losing her beloved father.

No-one could have been kinder or sweeter since her mother's death, and no-one, Romana thought, could have had a father who was so knowledgeable in all the things that were really interesting.

It had given her a sense of great pride that she had been able to help him ever since she was fifteen with his books.

He would have let Nicole help too, but she had laughed at the thought of her being capable of doing anything but dance.

"I can dance, and I can sing," she would say, "but, *non, non, Monsieur,* I am no good at *l'histoire,* or the books which you and Romana find so interesting. To me they are dull—very dull!"

She looked so pretty and entrancing as she spoke with

her French accent, that Romana had only kissed her and said:

"Nobody wants you to do anything but dance and sing, Nicole, and when you do both those things, you are irresistible!"

"I shall have to put up with one assistant, then," Mr. Wardell had said, "and if Romana cannot be with you as much as you wish, then that is your fault!"

"You must not be cruel, *Monsieur,* and make dear Romana work too hard," Nicole had protested.

She would often force Romana to forsake her books and ride with her over the fields, or dance with her on the lawn to the music played by the old village fiddler, who was completely captivated by her grace.

Nobody could have been more entrancing, more exciting or more lovely and because Nicole was the elder she was the leader in all their enterprises.

Romana never worried about her own looks but was content to admire and applaud her friend.

Only when the stage-coach was almost in London did Romana wonder if Nicole would be ashamed of her because her clothes were out of date. In fact, she had no idea what the fashion might be at this particular moment.

Her gowns were still full with a fichu over the shoulders and a sash around the waist.

At the last Posting Inn at which they had stopped there had been in the Dining-Room several elegantly dressed gentlemen with ladies who were very differently attired.

They had straight gowns with high waists that were almost transparent. Ribbons outlined their breasts and they wore high-crowned bonnets with pointed brims edged with lace.

Romana had gazed at them open-mouthed.

She had no idea that ladies would reveal so blatantly the curves of their figures, or that they could look so very different from the inhabitants of Little Hamble.

'If Mama had been alive I would have kept up with the latest vogue,' she thought. 'It is just that I have been so busy with Papa being ill and Nicole being away, that I fear she will think I look like Mrs. Noah.'

She cheered herself up with the thought that they would laugh together as they had always done, and nothing would matter.

'I am sure Nicole will lend me some of her old gowns,' Romana thought, 'until I can make enough money to buy new clothes for myself.'

Nevertheless, she had felt a little apprehensive as she drove in the hackney-carriage to Chelsea.

Now she was certain that the elegant Gentleman with the hard eyes was looking disparagingly at her full skirts which were badly crumpled, having been crushed in a stage-coach for several days.

"You intend to stay here the night?" the Gentleman asked.

"If Nicole will . . have me," Romana answered. "I have . . nowhere else to . . go."

She felt suddenly nervous and afraid as she had not been before.

Suppose Nicole did not want her? Suppose after coming all this way she was not pleased to see her? What would she do? Where would she go?

She felt a sudden sense of panic sweep over her! Then just as she was about to ask how long it would be before she could see Nicole there was a knock on the door and a servant came in.

"Yes?"

There was an inescapable note of eagerness in the Gentleman's voice as he waited for the man to speak.

"He's collapsed, M'Lord."

"Good!"

There was a note of complete satisfaction in the Gentleman's voice, and now Romana was looking at him even more apprehensively than she had before.

So he was a Lord! Nicole had not written home about meeting anyone so important as a gentleman of title.

In fact, now she came to think of it, Nicole had mentioned very few people by name in the letters she had written to her father and mother.

She had just talked about the School, about the comfortable accommodation she had found in Chelsea, and she had certainly not said a house, a whole house, was hers.

What was happening? Romana wondered. What did it all mean?

Unconsciously she clasped her hands together, and there was a beseeching expression in her eyes as she raised them to the Gentleman.

He was just about to leave the room, when he looked back at her with his eyes narrowing. Then he said:

"You say you are an orphan. Who knows you are here? Have you a Guardian?"

"N . no," Romana replied, "but Nicole's father and mother knew I was coming, and I explained . . everything in my letter."

"Stay here!" he said sharply, as if she had any intention of leaving.

Then he went out of the room, closing the door behind him.

After that, Romana thought, she could not bear even to remember what had happened, but she had to face the truth.

It *had* happened, and that was why she was here alone in a strange house with a man who had cursed her, who when the servant had thrown her out onto the pavement had picked her up and conveyed her in his carriage to this large and overwhelming house.

"What shall I do? What shall I do?" she wondered.

After what seemed a very long time the door of the room opened.

She felt her heart give a frightened thump as the Marquis came in accompanied by another man.

He walked towards her and because she felt he expected it of her, she rose to her feet. But she still kept her head bent, shadowing her face with the brim of her old-fashioned straw bonnet.

The two men advanced and the Marquis glanced at Mr. Barnham as if inviting him to speak first.

"Please sit down," he said. "I think it would be helpful if we had a talk, and if you could explain to us what happened last night."

Romana sat down gratefully because her legs suddenly

seemed very weak and not capable of supporting her.

She supposed she ought to say something, but when she tried to do so, she felt as if her voice had died in her throat.

"Perhaps I should explain," Mr. Barnham said in a kindly tone, "that I am the Marquis's secretary, and I look after His Lordship's affairs. He has told me, and I have seen a Certificate, as you must have, of your marriage. As you must have realised, he was unconscious at the time, so I must ask you to tell us what happened."

Still there was silence. Then in a frightened little voice they could hardly hear, Romana said:

"P . please . . if you could . .just give me . . a little m . money I . . I could go home. I . . I am afraid the stage-coach costs . . £3, but I could m . manage with that . . and just a f . few shillings for something to . . eat."

"And where is home?" Mr. Barnham asked.

"Little Hamble."

"That is where Nicole de Prêt told me she came from," the Marquis interposed.

"We were friends. That is why I c . came to her in . . London."

"She is your friend, and is your—profession the same as hers?" the Marquis enquired.

There was a pause before the word 'profession' and Mr. Barnham gave a slight frown before he interposed:

"His Lordship is asking if you are a dancer, as Miss de Prêt is at Covent Garden?"

"Nicole de Prêt is . . engaged at a . . Dancing-School," Romana said.

"Is that what she told you?" the Marquis asked, "or are you as big a liar as she is?"

He spoke harshly, and Romana gave a terrified start. Mr. Barnham saw that her fingers were linked together until the knuckles were white.

"I think, My Lord," he said in a quiet voice, "the young lady is trying to explain to us what happened, as best she can, and perhaps it has been as uncomfortable an experience for her as it has been for Your Lordship."

"You can hardly expect me to believe that," the Marquis said. "However, carry on, Barnham."

"How did you get to London?" Mr. Barnham asked Romana.

"By . . stage-coach," she replied, then with a little gasp she said:

"Do you . . think I could possibly . . have a glass of . . water? M . my throat is very . . dry."

"But of course," Mr. Barnham said. "I imagine you have had no breakfast."

"I . . I do not . . want anything to . . eat," Romana said quickly. "It is . . just that I am very . . thirsty . . and last night they gave me . . nothing . . not that I . . wanted anything."

Mr. Barnham walked across the room, opened the door and Romana heard him say to somebody outside:

"Bring coffee quickly, and arrange for breakfast for the young lady."

The servant must have hurried away to do his bidding and Mr. Barnham came back to sit down opposite Romana, to say quietly:

"I do not want to worry you until you have had something sustaining to eat, but you can understand that His Lordship has been through a very unpleasant and, if I may so, almost criminal experience, and as you are the only person who knows exactly what happened, we are obliged to question you."

"I . . understand that," Romana said. "It was . . horrible . . and very . . very . . wrong . . I knew that . . but there was . . n . nothing I could do about it."

"What do you mean—there was nothing you could do?" the Marquis asked sharply. "You could have refused to marry me! I was incapable of making the responses, and if you had refused to make them too, there would have been no marriage."

He spoke accusingly and for a moment there was silence. Then Romana said:

"I . . I d . did try to . . refuse."

"What do you mean—you tried?" the Marquis asked. "You had only to say you would not do it—it was not very difficult."

"I believe I . . did say that," Romana insisted, "but . . he

50

. . he hit me . . and I am . . a . . coward."

"Hit you?" Mr. Barnham asked.

For the first time since they had entered the room Romana raised her head.

It was still shadowed by the brim of her bonnet, but both the men could see quite clearly that on the very pale skin of her white cheek there was a huge red patch already turning purple at the edges.

It was the imprint of a hand; a hand that must have struck with all its force against someone small and frail, and inevitably have knocked her to the ground.

There was no need for either of them to speak, in fact, they could only stare at the evidence of their own eyes.

Romana lowered her face again.

"I . . I . . am . . sorry," she said almost inaudibly and fell forward at their feet.

CHAPTER THREE

As Romana collapsed on the floor both the Marquis and Mr. Barnham started to their feet. The latter knelt down beside her saying:

"She's fainted, I cannot think why the coffee has taken so long in coming."

As he spoke he looked up at the Marquis and was startled by the expression on his face. Then he looked back again at Romana and understood.

She was lying in an untidy heap with her face turned sideways so the huge purple mark on her right cheek was very prominent. Her old-fashioned bonnet had been knocked sidewards and her dress crumpled and travel-stained made her look as the Marquis had thought she might be, a servant girl!

Mr. Barnham heard the Marquis murmur:

"I will go and find the coffee."

He went from the room and Mr. Barnham put his arms around Romana. He was about to lift her up on to the sofa when another thought came to him. Instead he carried her in his arms towards the door.

As he reached it a servant with a tray of coffee opened it from the other side.

"Follow me upstairs," Mr. Barnham said sharply, "and bring a decanter of brandy."

He carried Romana, still unconscious, up the stairs and walked along the wide corridor which led to the best bedrooms.

He deliberately chose one in which the Marquis's most distinguished guests stayed and was about to try to open the door with Romana in his arms when he heard footsteps behind him.

He turned round to see that the Housekeeper, Mrs. Mayfield, had been following him.

"I heard you had brought a lady upstairs, Sir," she said with what Mr. Barnham knew was curiosity in her voice.

"The young lady's fainted," Mr. Barnham replied, "and as she has had an accident I thought, Mrs. Mayfield, that you should put her to bed."

"She will be staying here, Sir?"

"Yes," Mr. Barnham replied firmly, "she will be staying here."

"I heard the lady had brought a trunk with her," Mrs. Mayfield remarked.

Mr. Barnham thought a little dryly that news travelled fast in Sarne House as it did in every household where the servants were always aware of what was taking place.

He laid Romana very carefully down on the bed with Mrs. Mayfield assisting him by taking away her bonnet which was held by the ribbons that were still fastened round her neck.

When he could see Romana's face against the pillows Mr. Barnham was startled by her pallor against which the bruise on her face appeared almost brutally disfiguring.

He looked at her a little helplessly and Mrs. Mayfield said:

"Leave her to me, Sir. As the young lady has had an accident it is natural for her to be overcome by the shock of it, and if there's no other injury besides the one on her cheek, she'll be all right. But perhaps it'll be wise to send for a Physician?"

"Please discuss it with me later," Mr. Barnham suggested.

"I'll do that, Sir," Mrs. Mayfield said, "and would you be kind enough to hurry one of them men-servants upstairs with the coffee and the brandy which I heard you order."

"I will do that," Mr. Barnham replied.

He went downstairs in search of the Marquis and found him, as he expected, sitting in the Library which was the room he habitually used when he was alone.

It was a very fine room, decorated in pale green, the

53

cornice picked out in gold, and the books which covered the walls gave them a kaleidescope of colour which was singularly attractive.

Mr. Barnham however, at the moment could see nothing but the Marquis's expression of despair and despondency as he sat at his desk, his chin resting on his hands.

He had been waiting for his secretary and as Mr. Barnham shut the door behind him and walked across the room, he said:

"I cannot stand it, Barnham! It is utterly and completely impossible for me to produce a creature of that sort and present her to the world as the Marchioness of Sarne!"

Mr. Barnham knew by the raw note in his voice and the manner in which he spoke exactly what he was feeling.

It suddenly struck him that at the age of thirty-seven he had, as it were, acquired a family of two young people who needed his help more desperately than any children of his own might have done.

He chose his words with care before he said quietly:

"I think we have already agreed, My Lord, that you have no other alternative except to play straight into Lord Kirkhampton's hands."

"How can you be sure of that? If I send her away to Ireland, Scotland, anywhere in the world where she will not be seen by my friends, what could Kirkhampton do about it?"

"Accuse you of disposing of your wife! He might even suggest, although he would have to prove it, murder! And he could certainly start a witch-hunt in search of the missing Marchioness and perhaps offer a prize to the first person to discover her hiding place!"

"Good God!" the Marquis ejaculated. "Are you really suggesting Kirkhampton would go to such lengths?"

"I know the way His Lordship's mind works," Mr. Barnham said, "and I am certain he will never rest until he humiliates you to the point where, as far as he is concerned, you are on your knees!"

"He has done that already!" the Marquis said bitterly.

"Only if you allow him to do so," Mr. Barnham replied.

"How can I do anything else if I have to lug that creature

about with me as the Marchioness of Sarne? Can you not hear what my friends will say about her, let alone my enemies?"

Mr. Barnham did not speak for a moment and then he said slowly as he sat down in a chair:

"I am surprised, My Lord. I have never known you before to funk a fence."

The Marquis sat bolt upright and glared at him, and there was a long pause before he demanded:

"Are you accusing me, Barnham of cowardice?"

"I am not accusing you of anything, My Lord. I am only suggesting what I said before, that if we face the facts and decide how best we can circumvent and, if possible, beat Lord Kirkhampton at his own game!"

The Marquis brought his fist down heavily on his desk making the crystal and gold ink-pot rattle.

"Curse Kirkhampton!" he said violently. "May he rot in hell!"

"The only difficulty, My Lord," Mr. Barnham replied dryly, "is to get him there!"

Unexpectedly the Marquis laughed.

"All right, Barnham," he said, "you win! What I would do without you I cannot think. We will play the game your way and God help us all if it is as disastrous as I imagine it will be!"

"And now will you listen to my suggestions, My Lord?" Mr. Barnham enquired.

The Marquis inclined his head.

"I suggest," Mr. Barnham said, "that you leave immediately for Sarne. It is essential that none of your friends should find you here today or be able to communicate with you."

"Why?" the Marquis asked.

"Because tomorrow morning the announcement that your marriage has taken place, very quietly owing to deep mourning, will appear in the *Gazette*!"

The Marquis's lips tightened but he did not speak.

"If anyone calls here I shall decline all knowledge of where you might be on your Honeymoon," Mr. Barnham continued, "but I will join you either tomorrow or the following day, if she is well enough to travel, with—your wife."

There was just a slight pause before he said the last two words and he knew the Marquis shivered as he heard them.

"In the meantime," Mr. Barnham continued, "I have a great deal to do and I intend to spend a great deal of your money, so the sooner you leave me to my self-appointed task, the better!"

He rose to his feet saying as he did so:

"You will announce to the household at Sarne that you are married, and that Her Ladyship who is indisposed owing to an accident, will be joining you as soon as possible. There will be no celebrations, no festivities until she is completely recovered in health."

The Marquis groaned.

He was well aware of the sort of festivities his employees on the Estate, his farmers and tenants, would expect on such an auspicious occasion.

A huge dinner in the Tithe Barn; fireworks; presentations of presents; while his neighbours in the County would be all agog with curiosity to see his bride.

For the first time in his life the Marquis was unsure of himself, afraid of the consequences of any action he might make.

Always in the past, life had smiled on him and he had grown so used to being the victor, to winning the race, receiving the prize, accepting the applause and congratulations, that it was if suddenly he found himself naked and unprotected, like a blind man in a snow-storm, and had not the least idea what to do about it.

Mr. Barnham reached the door and turned back to smile at him.

"Do not despair," he said, "it might be much better than you expect, and on second thoughts I shall make every endeavour to bring Her Ladyship to you tomorrow. It would be a great mistake if Lord Kirkhampton should become aware, even inadvertently, that you were apart even for twenty-four hours."

"It would be better if you allowed me to kill him now, without further ado!" the Marquis said.

"It would inevitably mean your being exiled abroad for

several years," Mr. Barnham said, "and quite frankly I have not much hope that this armistice with Napoleon will last more than a year, if that."

The Marquis looked surprised and then he laughed again, though the sound had little humour in it.

"So I have a choice," he said, "of either being a prisoner of Napoleon or the husband of some creature Kirkhampton picked up in the streets, who doubtless eats with her fingers and whose only accomplishment is knowing how to milk a cow!"

Mr. Barnham was just about to protest that, if nothing else, the woman he had married had an educated voice. Then he thought it would be best for the Marquis to discover any virtues she might have for himself.

He was well aware that at the moment, blinded with hatred for Lord Kirkhampton, he was revolted by the appearance of the woman to whom he was married.

He could see nothing in her but his own degradation and humiliation, but that was not to say that he might not change his mind later on!

When Mr. Barnham saw Romana lying pale and unconscious on the bed to which he had carried her, he had realised she had not the appearance either of a prostitute or of the servant the Marquis had suggested her to be.

But it was too soon to be sure of anything, and in the Marquis's present mood Mr. Barnham knew it would be best first to accept the circumstances for what they were, and then to be grateful for small mercies as he found them.

He went at once to his own office and sat down to write quickly several notes to the most exclusive shops in Bond Street.

It was not difficult for him to know where the Ladies of Quality and the more expensive cocottes bought their clothes.

Mr. Barnham had paid an enormous number of bills on behalf of the Marquis, for gowns, shawls, bonnets, gloves, negligees and all the other frivolities which made up an attractive woman's wardrobe.

He knew that the notes he sent out by the grooms from Sarne House would be answered eagerly and quickly by their recipients.

He had just finished this task when Mrs. Mayfield came into the office.

"I was expecting you, Mrs. Mayfield," Mr. Barnham said. "How is the young lady?"

"She's better now, Sir," Mrs. Mayfield replied. "She's still somewhat shocked and I'm wondering what can have happened to her."

Mr. Barnham knew Mrs. Mayfield was consumed with curiosity and he answered:

"Please do not press her to confide in you. I am sure it would be a mistake. And now, Mrs. Mayfield, I want your help."

"Of course, Sir. If there's anything I can do," Mrs. Mayfield began.

"There is a great deal," Mr. Barnham interrupted, and described in detail exactly what he required.

. . . . .

Travelling in the Marquis's fastest and most comfortable carriage the following day, Romana felt she was still dreaming.

But now the dream was no longer the terrible soul-destroying nightmare it had been since she had arrived in London.

It was still hard to credit that what was happening to her was real.

Yet the fact she was in a carriage drawn by four of the best bred horses she had ever seen, and sitting beside the gentleman who spoke to her in such a kindly and gentle manner, was somehow soothing after the turbulence in her mind which had made her feel at times she must be going insane.

Never, until she met Lord Kirkhampton, had Romana ever known real fear. Then on that terrible evening when she had arrived at Nicole's house in Chelsea, he had turned to her and said:

"I have a task for you and one which will doubtless in the future be to your advantage, if you have the sharpness to grasp at anything you can get out of it!"

"I . . I do . . not . . understand," Romana had said.

"You will!" Lord Kirkhampton retorted. "Stay here until I send for you."

He had gone from the small Sitting Room shutting the door behind him before Romana could ask him what he meant.

Then she had sat and waited, and waited, until she thought Lord Kirkhampton must have forgotten her very existence and Nicole could not have been told of her arrival.

She heard voices outside the door and was aware that Lord Kirkhampton was giving orders in a peremptory manner. She could even hear faintly the sound of a carriage driving away.

An hour later, it may have been more, the carriage must have returned for there was a sound of someone arriving and Lord Kirkhampton greeting them in the hall.

She wondered what it could all be about and longed to see Nicole to explain why she was so late, and also to say how sorry she was to arrive at such an inconvenient hour.

'It was not my fault,' she said to herself, 'but if Nicole is entertaining, she will not want me to meet her friends when I am looking like this.'

Because her head was aching after the long journey she took off her bonnet and smoothed her hair into place in front of a small mirror which was hanging on one of the walls.

'Tomorrow,' Romana told her reflection, 'I must try to find a more fashionable style in which to arrange my hair.'

Quite suddenly she wished she had not come to London.

It had been a mistake and if Nicole did not want her the best thing she could do was to go back to Little Hamble and stay with one of the villagers until she could write to some of her relatives and ask if she could visit them.

Her father had several elderly cousins living in various parts of England.

She had never heard from them except occasionally at Christmas and Romana knew that most of them were not well off and would doubtless resent an extra mouth to feed in their households even if she could make herself useful.

Her mother on the other hand had several relatives in far

better circumstances, but they had never bothered about her until her death.

Then they had sent rather stiff and formal letters of condolence to her father which were obviously more of a duty than written from their hearts.

Her mother's family had never considered the marriage a particularly advantageous one in the first place and, she had therefore been too proud to keep in touch with those of her family who were not prepared to appreciate her husband.

"There must be someone amongst them who would like to have me," Romana told herself.

At the same time she did not feel very optimistic!

The door opened behind her and she turned round with a little start.

"I am ready for you," Lord Kirkhampton said.

There was an expression on his face which made her feel instinctively that what he was about to suggest would be unpleasant.

But there was nothing she could do but go with him as he obviously expected and she followed him up the stairs to the first floor.

He walked ahead of her and opened the door into a Drawing Room where there was another room, but Romana had eyes only for Nicole.

She was standing at the far end by the fireplace, looking very lovely and very elegant.

For a moment Romana thought it could not really be the same girl she had treated as a sister and with whom she had shared lessons, romped in the garden and ridden over the fields.

With a little cry of delight she ran towards her, and Nicole put her arms around her.

"Nicole! Nicole!" she cried, "it is so wonderful to see you!"

Nicole held her close, then she said:

"Dearest Romana, I only received your letter this morning. Why, oh why did you have to come here today, of all days?"

Romana looked at her wide-eyed.

"What is wrong, dearest?" she asked. "If you do not . . want me . . I will go . . back."

"It ees not that," Nicole said in a nervous voice. "It is just that now His Lordship has seen you, there ees something he . . wishes you to . . do."

She glanced over Romana's shoulder as she spoke and, as if he was impatient at the exchange of greetings between the two friends, Lord Kirkhampton walked towards them, saying sharply:

"Let us get on with what has to be done, and get that swine out of the way!"

"Please, Milor', change your mind," Nicole pleaded. "Eet ees wrong! You know eet ees wrong, and I do not wish my friend, Romana, to be involved."

"We have discussed this already," Lord Kirkhampton said in a lofty voice. "I do not intend to argue any further, Nicole. As for your friend, she should be grateful!"

Romana looked at him in surprise as he went on:

"You tell me she is penniless and looking for a job. Then what better position can we find her than to be the wife of Sarne?"

Romana was looking at him in a bewildered fashion when she heard Nicole say beside her:

"I am sorry . . dearest Romana. I do not . . mean thees to . . happen . . perhaps His Lordship ees right and it will be to your advantage in the end."

"What are you . . talking about?" Romana enquired. "I . . do not understand."

She knew by the expression on Nicole's face that she was perturbed and not far from tears.

She had known Nicole all her life: the mere suggestion of a quarrel would leave her limp and helpless, sobbing despairingly. She was afraid this might happen now and almost protectively she put out her hands towards her.

"Please do not be—angry," Nicole pleaded.

"About what?" Romana questioned.

"Then let me make it clear to you," Lord Kirkhampton said. "You are to be married! Married to that gentleman over there who is not at the moment in a condition to be aware of it!"

The tone in which Lord Kirkhampton spoke was both mocking and unpleasant, and there was a jeering note in his voice which made Romana wince.

She thought for a moment that he must be joking.

Then looking in the direction in which he was pointing she saw collapsed in a chair, his hands hanging limp on either side of it, his legs thrust out in front of him, a man!

She stared at him thinking his attitude was very strange. Then she looked at the other person in the room.

It was a Parson! There was no mistaking that! He wore a long black cassock with two white muslin bands at his throat.

He had an unpleasant appearance and there was something almost evil-looking about his face. Then the full impact of what Lord Kirkhampton had said made Romana ask:

"What are you saying? I have no intention of marrying anyone! You must be mistaken."

"I am not mistaken," Lord Kirkhampton replied, "and you are to marry now, immediately. I suggest you make no fuss about it, if you know what is good for you."

Romana gave a little cry.

"Nicole!" she said appealingly.

To her astonishment her friend released her hand and turned her back on her, although Romana was aware that she had drawn out a handkerchief and was holding it to her eyes.

"Nicole, Nicole!" she cried frantically, "this cannot . . happen to . . me!"

She moved to her friend's side, holding onto her arm.

"Do as you are told . . Romana," Nicole said through her tears. "There ees . . nothing I can say to . . prevent it."

Romana looked round wildly, as if for a way of escape, but the door was on the other side of the room. If she ran towards it she had to pass Lord Kirkhampton.

As if he read her thoughts he reached out his hand and took hold of her wrist.

"Come along now," he said. "There is no time for dramatics or girlish reluctance. As it happens, there is not a woman in London who would not give her eyes to be in your position—to be married to Sarne, despite the fact that he is the biggest God-damned villain that ever breathed!"

Lord Kirkhampton almost spat out the words, but Romana was hardly listening. Instead she was trying to twist her wrist free of his grip.

Inevitably he was far too strong for her. He dragged her across the room until she stood beside the chair in which the Marquis lay unconscious.

"Come along, Parson," Lord Kirkhampton said, "and get along with the Service. I will make the responses for the bridegroom. The bride can speak for herself."

"It is irregular . . ." the Parson murmured but almost beneath his breath.

"You have been paid enough to marry Satan himself," Lord Kirkhampton retorted. "Now do not let us waste any more time."

The Parson opened his book and moved a few steps so that he could stand in front of the unconscious man and herself. Romana gave a cry.

"You must all be . . crazy!" she said. "I will not be . . married in such a . . fashion. It is wrong . . it is blasphemous, and I have no . . intention of . . tieing myself to a man I do not . . know or . . love."

She felt as if Lord Kirkhampton and the Priest were paying no attention to her, and she said again:

"I will not . . make the . . responses. Nothing . . shall make . . me!"

Lord Kirkhampton did not reply in words.

He was holding Romana's wrist in his left hand, and now he raised his right and brought his open palm down against her cheek with a resounding crack which seemed to echo around the room.

What was more, the force of his blow made her stagger and she went down on one knee and would have fallen if he had not been holding her.

She gave a cry both of fear and pain.

"You . . hit me!" she exclaimed almost childishly.

"And I will do so again," Lord Kirkhampton said, "if you continue to defy me."

He raised his hand as he spoke, at the same time dragging

Romana to her feet.

Because she felt almost stupid from the blow he had given her and also terrified in a manner she had never been terrified before, her voice seemed to die in her throat.

It was impossible to go on fighting—impossible not to do as she was told.

As if Lord Kirkhampton knew she was now subdued and submissive he dropped his right hand, but he still held Romana by the wrist and she knew that he was only waiting to hit her again.

Already her cheek from the first blow, was throbbing and burning in a manner which was exceedingly painful.

The Parson opened his prayer-book.

He ignored the introductory prayers and started the Service with the words:

"Wilt thou Vallient Alexander take Romana to be your wedded wife?"

"I will," Lord Kirkhampton said, in a voice that seemed to be almost a trumpet-call of triumph for a fallen enemy.

"Romana, wilt thou take this man for thy wedded husband?"

Just for a moment Romana thought she must protest again. She could not let this thing happen to her. She could not be married to a man she did not know, and worse still, who was not aware of what was happening to him.

She knew it was wrong—she knew the Parson performing the Service was an evil man, far from good or holy, and that everything had been purposely engineered, deriving from the hatred she could feel emanating in a horrible manner from the man who held her captive.

Then as the Parson waited for her response and she wanted to say that nothing would make her submit to being married in such circumstances, she felt Lord Kirkhampton's fingers tightening on her wrist until it hurt, and once again he raised his right hand.

Even as she despised herself for being a coward, even as every instinct in her body cried out against her yielding to physical fear, Romana heard her own voice, trembling and weak, whisper:

"I . . will."

Now driving away from London to an unknown destination she told herself that somehow she must escape, although how, and where she could go, she had no idea.

She only knew that mixed indivisibly in her mind were the violence of Lord Kirkhampton, the harsh manner in which the Marquis had spoken to her on coming downstairs this morning, and the way in which he had refused to listen to her when she had pleaded with him for help.

She had been as frightened of him then as she had been frightened of Lord Kirkhampton on the night before.

She felt it was only through the intervention and the kindness of the man sitting beside her that she had not been physically assaulted by the man to whom she had been united in matrimony.

'He hates me! He will hurt me when he can!' she thought and shivered.

"You are not cold?" Mr. Barnham asked.

"No, no!" Romana said quickly. "It is quite a warm day, and I have this beautiful shawl to wear."

Yesterday afternoon, having slept after being given food and something warm to drink, she had been awakened by Mrs. Mayfield to ask if the dressmakers could take her measurements.

"They'll not tire you, Miss," she said, "they have just been ordered by His Lordship to make some clothes for you. It'll be easier for them if they have your measurements correctly to start with."

Still half-asleep Romana had found it too much effort to ask why His Lordship should wish to give her clothes, except she knew that she certainly needed them.

His behaviour up until now had certainly not seemed benevolent or in any way kindly, but she was too exhausted to question anything more that happened.

Merely because Mrs. Mayfield expected it and was ready to help her, she stepped out of bed and stood in her nightgown while three dressmakers who had come into the room, complimented her on the elegance of her figure.

Then she was allowed to get back into bed.

She had in fact been astonished when later that evening

Mrs. Mayfield had brought a number of gowns into the room to hang them up in the wardrobe.

"I understand, Miss, you'll be going to the country first thing in the morning with Mr. Barnham," she said. "It would be a pity to crease these pretty gowns, so I'll not pack them until the very last moment."

Romana had looked wide-eyed at what she held up for her inspection.

But she was still too bemused to want to ask many questions.

It was only after breakfast had been brought to her in bed at what seemed to her a very late hour that she learnt a great many more clothes had arrived, but they were not being unpacked, but loaded on a Landau which was leaving for the country ahead of hers.

"There's a very pretty pale blue travelling-gown I thought you'd like to wear, Miss," Mrs. Mayfield said, "and a lovely bonnet trimmed with roses to go with it."

When she saw them, Romana could not help a little thrill of excitement run through her, but as she did so, she remembered who was paying for them and felt her heart throb with a sudden fear.

"What is bothering you?" Mr. Barnham asked now in his quiet voice.

"It is . . nothing," she replied.

He knew she was shivering again and he thought that her hands in their smart suede gloves were trembling.

"There is nothing to frighten you," he said. "Sarne is certainly very impressive, in fact one of the most impressive houses in England. The Marquis's mother, the late Marchioness, made it very comfortable and very beautiful inside. It is a home, which so many houses in the same category, do not manage to be."

"It will not be my home," Romana wanted to say.

But she told herself that it was a mistake to argue about anything that was said, as she had learnt from Lord Kirkhampton.

The mark on her cheek was surprisingly better. The redness had gone because Mrs. Mayfield had applied a soothing salve which she said took the inflamation out of anything.

There was however undoubtedly a bruise from Lord Kirkhampton's fingers, but the worst of this had been skilfully covered this morning with a cream which Mrs. Mayfield said came from Bond Street, after which she had applied a thick layer of powder.

"I . . I have never used powder before!" Romana protested.

"All Society ladies use cosmetics, Miss," Mrs. Mayfield had replied. "I'll add a little salve to your lips and a touch of rouge to your cheek which has not been injured, and no-one will notice the bruise, painful though it must still be."

"It certainly hurts to smile," Romana admitted.

But she thought it was unlikely she would want to smile considering the terrible things that had happened to her.

"What time am I leaving?" she asked when Mrs. Mayfield said her bath was ready.

"After luncheon Miss, when many more of your gowns will have arrived."

"Am I going . . alone?"

"Oh, no, Miss! Mr. Barnham will accompany you. His Lordship went to Sarne yesterday, so there'll only be two of you in the carriage, not that His Lordship ever cares for being 'cooped up', as he calls it."

It was a relief, Romana thought, that she had not to see the Marquis as soon as she went downstairs. At the same time, she dreaded reaching Sarne and having to see him there.

"I hate him!" she told herself. "He is as cruel and terrible as Lord Kirkhampton. How can Nicole, of all people, become involved with such frightening and wicked men?"

It seemed impossible that Nicole, who was so sweet and gentle, could have become so different so quickly.

How could she tolerate seeing her greatest friend, who was closer to her than any sister, married to a man who was as horrible as the Marquis of Sarne, and why did she have to take orders from Lord Kirkhampton.

Surely she was not beholden to him, when she was doing so well at the Dancing School and had enough money to send home to her parents.

It struck Romana again that the house in which Nicole lived was very luxurious for someone who was only a dancing-teacher.

She remembered that not only her gown had seemed very expensive last night, but there had been a diamond necklace round her neck, diamonds sparkling in her ears, and she had also worn a diamond bracelet.

Of course, they might have been false, but somehow it did not seem like Nicole to wear a profusion of jewellery that was not real.

Had Lord Kirkhampton given her such expensive presents? If so, why?

There seemed to be no answers to Romana's questions and they only made her more afraid of the future, more apprehensive of what was happening to herself.

If only, she thought bitterly, she had not come to London. If only she had stayed in Little Hamble, or written to her relations. But now it was too late.

She knew that while she had apparently trunkfuls of expensive clothes she did not possess any money.

They must have driven for a long time in silence until suddenly Mr. Barnham said:

"There is Sarne!"

Romana bent forward to look in the direction he pointed.

On the other side of the valley set against a background of green trees was the largest, most imposing and beautiful house she had ever seen in her life.

It was like a jewel, its perfect proportions reflected in a huge lake that filled the valley beneath.

For a moment Romana thought the loveliness of it seemed to fill her mind like a stanza of poetry. Then she remembered to whom it belonged.

'I shall be lost in a prison .. overwhelmed,' she thought in a sudden panic and wanted, as she had never wanted anything in her life before, to run away.

A little further down the road the horses turned in through two magnificent gold topped gates with stone lodges on either side of them.

There was a long tree-bordered drive, and all the time

they were descending it the house on the other side of the valley drew nearer and nearer.

It also seemed to grow bigger and bigger, until Romana thought that it menaced her, and she felt herself shrink into the corner of the carriage wishing she could slip away into insignificance and become invisible.

They crossed a fine three-arched bridge, then entered a court-yard in front of the central block of the house.

There was a long flight of stone steps leading up to a huge door flanked with Corinthian columns, and the sunshine seemed to gleam golden on a thousand windows.

Romana had seen that the Marquis's personal standard was flying against the sky.

"We are here!" Mr. Barnham said in a tone of satisfaction.

Romana wanted to cry out that she was afraid. She wanted to go on driving or even return to London.

A red carpet was spread on the steps and there were numerous flunkeys in knee-breeches and gold-braided livery with powdered wigs.

Mr. Barnham stepped out first then assisted Romana to alight.

"I forgot to tell you," he said in a low voice that only she could hear, "that at Sarne they have been told of your marriage to His Lordship, and you will be greeted as the Marchioness of Sarne."

Nothing could have frightened Romana more than she was already and she felt herself start and her heart thump unpleasantly.

The Groom-of-the-Chambers who was more resplendently dressed than the rest of the staff, was waiting in the Hall to say:

"Welcome, My Lady! I wish to convey on behalf of all the household at Sarne, our best wishes for your and His Lordship's happiness."

"Thank . . you," Romana managed to stammer.

Then the Groom-of-the-Chambers was walking ahead while with Mr. Barnham walking beside her, Romana followed him across a huge Hall with painted walls and a ceiling rioting with goddesses and cupids.

They moved through a long series of rooms all so large so overwhelming and grand that Romana was afraid to look at them.

Then at length after what seemed a very long walk, the Groom-of-the-Chambers stopped before two high doors, carved and painted exquisitely with gilded handles.

They stepped into what seemed to Romana to be an enormous room and he announced in stentorian tones:

"The Marchioness of Sarne, M'Lord, and Mr. Barnham!"

Romana drew in her breath. For a moment she thought it impossible for her feet to carry her any further. She was so afraid that she knew she was trembling.

She knew too that the thought of meeting the Marquis again was so terrifying, so repulsive, that she wished that the floor would open and swallow her up, or that she could die.

But her pride and her training in self-control since she was a child carried her forward, although it was impossible to raise her eyes towards the man she knew was waiting for her.

·　·　·　·　·

The Marquis had in fact, spent a restless and tortured night alone at Sarne.

He had risen early in the morning because it was impossible to sleep, to ride one of his most spirited and difficult horses until both he and the animal were tired out.

He had returned to the house to find it was impossible to eat the breakfast which was set in front of him, and instead he broke the rule of a lifetime and drank brandy instead of coffee.

He was far too anxious to be athletically fit ever to over-indulge in any respect and unlike his contemporaries and the Prince of Wales, was extremely abstemious.

But only brandy could relieve in a little way, his feeling of apprehension and horror at the trick that fate, or rather Lord Kirkhampton, had served him.

Today he was forced against his will to enter upon a matrimonial existence which he had always believed was something which lay far away in the unforeseen future, and would not confront him for a great number of years.

70

But now he was married—married to some common woman chosen for him by his greatest enemy! And circumstances being what they were, he had to school her into appearing with some semblance of dignity as the Marchioness of Sarne.

The Marquis was a realist, and he did not under-estimate the task that lay ahead of him!

While every instinct in him rebelled at the idea, he knew that Barnham was right in saying there was no other alternative except to defy Kirkhampton by anticipating what move he intended to take.

When the newspapers arrived at Sarne and he saw *The Times* and the *Morning Post* waiting for him in the great Library which contained over five thousand valuable books, he could not bring himself to pick them up and open them.

He knew that his secretary would not have forgotten to send the announcement of his marriage not only to the *London Gazette* but to all the other newspapers, even though they would copy it once it appeared.

Now the die was cast, the world would know that the most elusive and the most sought after bachelor of the *Beau Monde* had been caught at last, and as the country-folk used to put it, was 'leg-shackled'.

"Why in God's name did this have to happen to me?" the Marquis asked the portraits of his ancestors.

He asked the same question as he rode over the green acres which had been in the Sarne family for over five hundred years.

It was a question mankind had always asked in adversity and seldom found a satisfactory answer, and the Marquis returned home as frustrated and uneasy as he had been when he left.

He ate luncheon alone, but found it impossible to settle to anything during the afternoon.

He knew approximately the time at which Mr. Barnham would arrive and as he waited he tried to think what the woman he had married looked like.

But he could only remember a burning red bruise which seemed to make her face grotesque and her clothes, which

71

were so out of fashion as to be ludicrous.

He thought of his mother who had always been extremely elegant and had worn the Sarne diamonds like a Queen.

He could remember her standing at the top of the staircase when they gave a great Reception at Sarne House in London, and he could recall her in the Ballroom here receiving a thousand guests with a grace that ensured that every party at which she was the hostess was a resounding success from the moment it began.

It was what he would expect of his wife, and he told himself that the reason he had never married was that he had never found a woman who he admired or respected enough to put in his mother's place.

Now it was to be filled by some vulgar hobbledehoy peasant from the country!

Perhaps even there he was mistaken, and she was, in fact, nothing but the sweepings off the streets of London.

"Oh, God," he cried again for the thousandth time, "why did this happen to me?"

As if in a mocking response there was the Groom-of-the-Chambers' voice announcing "the Marchioness of Sarne and Mr. Barnham."

The woman was moving towards him! The Marquis forced himself with an almost violent effort, to look at her.

He saw she was not in the least what he had anticipated, robust and common. Instead she was delicate and graceful, with very large eyes which seemed to fill a small pointed face.

But to the Marquis's astonishment the expression in her eyes was one of fear and unmistakably, although he could hardly believe it, of hatred!

CHAPTER FOUR

Romana came down the stairs nervously wondering where she should go, and it was with a sense of relief that she saw the Groom-of-the-Chambers waiting for her in the Hall.

She was wearing one of the new gowns that had been bought for her in London and was, she thought, so beautiful, so elegant, that she should be wearing it at a Ball rather than for what she anticipated would be a quiet evening with the man who made her shiver even to think of him.

But everything that Mr. Barnham had ordered in London was so exquisite, so different from anything that Romana had ever owned before, that she felt as if they forced her to play a part that was not herself.

The Housekeeper had produced a maid who she said would look after her, and who had arranged her hair skilfully in a style that Romana had never seen previously.

It certainly became her, framing her small face and, she hoped, helping further to conceal the mark on her cheek.

Because Mrs. Mayfield had taught her how to do it, she applied the cream which had come from Bond Street, powdered it, and feeling she was being very daring added a touch of rouge and a little lip salve in what she had been told was the fashionable manner.

When she looked in the mirror she certainly thought she looked very unlike her usual self.

At the same time, she was aware that the fear she still felt inside her was showing in her eyes and she hoped that the Marquis would not be aware of how terrified she was of him.

The Groom-of-the-Chambers was bowing in front of her.

"Good-evening, Your Ladyship," he said, "I'm to escort you to the Silver Salon, where His Lordship's waiting."

Romana wanted to say that she wished she could go anywhere rather than encounter His Lordship again, but she knew whatever the circumstances in which she found herself, she must behave like a lady, as her mother and father would expect her to do.

She forced a little smile to her lips and followed the Groom-of-the-Chambers across the Hall.

The Silver Salon was not the room in which she had met the Marquis earlier in the afternoon where, when he had asked about her journey and Mr. Barnham had replied, he had suggested she might like to go to her room.

"You will have time to rest before dinner," he said in a tone which Romana thought was not particularly felicitous for her comfort.

But she had merely murmured "Thank you", and Mr. Barnham had taken her back to the Hall where the Groom-of-the-Chambers had led her upstairs.

He had handed her over to another housekeeper, who looked so like Mrs. Mayfield in her rustling black silk gown that they might almost have been twin sisters.

The Housekeeper at Sarne was called Mrs. Hughes, and she had been working on the estate, Romana learned, since the age of twelve.

She was obviously very proud of the house which she looked upon as her own home as well as that of the Marquis.

She chattered about the beauties of it while she was helping Romana to undress, quite unaware that the new Marchioness hated the very name of Sarne and wanted only to run away.

When Romana entered the Silver Salon she realised that it was a very impressive and beautifully decorated room with painted panels to match the ceiling and an Aubusson carpet with a pattern of flowers and blue ribbons.

But it was impossible to see anything very clearly except the Marquis standing waiting for her with his back to the marble fireplace, looking frighteningly large and over-whelming and at the same time, in his evening clothes, extremely elegant.

He was alone and Romana had hoped that Mr. Barnham would be there but she forced herself to walk slowly and gracefully towards him, dropping him a small curtsey when she reached his side.

"You will have a glass of champagne?" the Marquis asked.

Romana realised that a footman had followed her into the room and was offering it to her on a silver tray.

She was about to shake her head, then she thought perhaps the champagne would give her some 'Dutch courage', so she took a glass and sipped it delicately.

Another servant refilled the empty glass the Marquis held in his hand and Romana wondered if he felt the need for courage as much as she did herself.

Then she told herself that whatever he felt would reflect his horrible nature and she bent her head so that she would not have to look at him. After a moment he said in an irritated tone:

"Dinner is late! If there is one thing I really dislike, it is unpunctuality!"

Even as he spoke the Butler announced from the doorway:

"Dinner is served, My Lady!"

Romana started as he spoke and realised for the first time that she was now ostensibly the mistress of Sarne.

Because the idea was so frightening she put down her hardly touched glass of champagne on a small table, hoping the Marquis would not be aware that her hand was trembling.

He was, however, not looking at her but merely moved forward a few paces to offer her his arm.

Because she had no wish to touch him, she put her fingers very lightly on the arm he offered her and they walked towards the door.

She thought as they went down a wide corridor that she could feel waves of anger emanating from him and wondered if he in return, was aware of her feelings.

The Dining-Room was smaller than she had expected and she guessed that there would also be a big Banqueting Hall which would not be used except on formal occasions.

As the Marquis led her towards the table she saw it was decorated with white flowers, and thought that the servants had done this to celebrate their marriage. She was quite sure the idea had not been initiated by the bridegroom.

He seated himself at the head of the table and Romana found that she was seated on the side rather than facing him at the other end.

She thought wildly that even the proximity was unpleasant, then she told herself severely that she must behave with propriety.

It would be in extremely bad taste and certainly undignified to let the servants realise how much she and her husband disliked each other.

However they might behave in private, in public they must keep up some sort of appearance of politeness, if nothing else.

Romana almost felt as if her mother was telling her what to do, and she knew, however horrible the circumstances in which she found herself, she must try to behave like a lady even if the Marquis did not behave like a gentleman.

The first course was soup, and as the servants moved aside Romana forced herself to say:

"This is a very . . charming room . . but I expect you have a . . larger one for when you give . . parties."

Her voice sounded small even to herself and she thought the Marquis looked at her as if he was surprised that she had spoken at all.

After a moment's pause he replied:

"That is true. I do not use the larger State Rooms when I am alone."

"It is . . pleasant to be able to . . choose," Romana said.

"Exactly!" he replied.

There was silence and she thought he was making it unnecessarily difficult. At the same time she would not let him defeat her.

"The horses which . . brought me here from . . London I thought were very . . fine," she said. "Do you . . breed

76

them?"

"No. As a matter of fact I bought that particular team from a friend of mine who, because he lost so much money gambling, had to dispose of his stable."

"That must have been very sad for him."

"I am sure it was," the Marquis agreed, "but people should not gamble if they cannot afford to do so."

Romana had an impulse to argue with him, just for the sake of arguing.

She wanted to say it was very easy for people who were rich to condemn those who were poor for gaming, for whom sometimes all they had left was the hope that somehow fortune would smile on them.

But it was difficult anyway to talk to a man who obviously had no wish to talk to her, so she allowed a little time to elapse before she asked if the trout they were eating had been caught in the lake.

"I imagine so," the Marquis replied.

"Do you fish . . yourself?"

"When I have the time, which is not often."

Romana gave a little sigh.

She was disliking him more every moment and it was no consolation to know that he was as exasperated with the situation as she was.

Course after course was brought in by the servants only to be sent away almost untouched, and it was a relief when dinner was finished, the dessert was put on the table and the Marquis refused a glass of port.

"I will have brandy," he said to the Butler.

As soon as a glass had been set before him the servants bowed and withdrew.

This, Romana knew, was when she too, could be free.

"I think I should . . leave you . . My Lord," she said, and rose to her feet.

She had a feeling he was surprised that she knew how to behave, but he replied:

"If you will go into the Silver Salon where we met before dinner, I will join you in a few minutes. I think it is time we had a talk together."

Romana inclined her head and walked towards the door.

77

To her surprise the Marquis made no effort to open it for her, only slumping back in his chair to raise his glass of brandy to his lips.

She opened the door for herself and walked down the corridor with her head high, telling herself as she did so, that her mother would be proud of her and however boorish the Marquis might be, she would not allow him to defeat her.

At the same time, while she waited in the Silver Salon she felt her defiance giving way to apprehension, and every moment that she was alone seemed to make her more nervous and more afraid.

She looked at the valuable *objets d'art* on the tables around the room and thought that while every one of them was worth large sums of money, she had not a penny with which she could escape from this ostentatious prison and go back to where she belonged.

She had a longing for her home that was almost like a physical pain in her breast.

It was no longer hers but she thought even to be in the village amongst the people she had known ever since she was a child, would be a happiness beyond words, rather than be here surrounded by splendour and hatred.

"The Marquis hates me, and I hate him!" she told herself. "Somehow we must do something about it. I cannot go on living like this."

The thought of the future was so appalling that she could not contemplate it.

Then the door opened and the Marquis came into the Salon.

She felt her heart constrict in a kind of terror and it was only with a superhuman effort that she managed to move from the table where she had been standing, to sit down on the edge of a chair by the fireplace.

He came towards her and she saw he was carrying a glass of brandy, and thought disdainfully that she was not surprised that he drank. It was in keeping with her whole opinion of him.

The Marquis put his glass down on the marble mantle-piece and leaned against it to look down at her.

She had a feeling that he had been planning what he should say, for he began immediately:

"I think we should discuss the future together. I suppose you have some idea of what you want to do and what you require?"

The tone of his voice was unpleasant and she had the feeling that he expected her to make demands upon him.

"I require . . nothing," she said hastily.

"Come now, you can hardly expect me to believe that," the Marquis replied. "I imagine Kirkhampton pointed out to you very clearly the advantages you would gain from being my wife."

For the first time since it happened Romana remembered Lord Kirkhampton saying:

"I have a task for you, and one which will doubtless in the future bring you many advantages, if you have the sharpness to grasp at anything you can get out of it."

She had not understood what he meant, but now she supposed he had been referring to the fact that she would be the Marchioness of Sarne.

As if the Marquis read her thoughts, he said sharply:

"I thought Kirkhampton would make it very clear to you if you had not thought it out for yourself, which I am sure you had! Well then, what do you want? You might as well tell me now."

"I want . . nothing," Romana said, "except if it were possible . . not to be married . . not to be . . here."

The Marquis laughed and it was not a very pleasant sound.

"You can hardly expect me to believe that. Kirkhampton and your little friend Nicole de Prêt set up a very ingenious trap for me, and I was fool enough to fall into it."

"I am sure Nicole had . . nothing to do with it," Romana retorted.

She remembered how unhappy and frightened Nicole had seemed and she was sure that when Lord Kirkhampton struck her she had heard Nicole's voice cry out in protest.

"On the contrary," the Marquis objected angrily, "she had everything to do with it. She was the bait, and I admit I fell for it, hook, line and sinker!"

He made a sound of sheer fury before he went on:

79

"I should have been suspicious of course, when she insisted that we had supper at her house instead of going out somewhere, and while I drank my own drugged claret I presume you and Kirkhampton were hiding in a cupboard, waiting to pounce on me the moment I was unconscious."

There was so much fury in his voice that Romana, afraid he might stifle her, shrank back a little further in her chair.

He was not looking at her however, but staring across the room with his fists clenched.

"You must have been laughing," he went on, "laughing at a greenhorn who could not sense danger, but walked blindly into a pit of destruction."

Romana did not speak and after a moment he said:

"Well, your plot succeeded and now you had better tell me the worst. I thought when I first saw you, you were a servant. Looking at you now, I presume you are a prostitute, like your friend."

The contempt in his voice swept away for a moment Romana's fear of him and left only her anger.

"How dare you say such things about Nicole!" she exclaimed. "How dare you insinuate that she is anything but good and pure, as she has always been!"

Romana rose to her feet as she spoke, as if she felt she must confront the Marquis.

As she faced him he looked down at her in surprise, then it was swept away in an expression of mocking cynicism.

"So that is your game, is it?" he asked. "Ignorance! Well, I am not falling for that old story. Of course Nicole is a harlot, as you know and I know. She is living with Kirkhampton and has doubtless lived with dozens of men before. . . ."

He got no further for Romana interrupted him.

"How dare you say such things!" she cried. "It is untrue, it is wrong and wicked! I will not listen to such lies!"

She turned as she spoke and began to run across the room towards the door.

She had nearly reached it when it opened and Mr. Barnham came into the Salon.

"Excuse me, My Lord . . ." he began, but he got no further.

Romana flung herself against him saying frantically:

"Take me away! Take me away! I cannot stay . . here with that wicked . . evil . . man!"

Mr. Barnham put his arm round Romana to support her and looked across the room towards the Marquis as if for an explanation.

Before he could speak, before he could do anything more, Romana burst into tears.

She had not cried last night. She had managed to control her feelings all day, but now her fear of the Marquis and the horror of what he had been saying broke down her last defences.

She cried tempestuously and helplessly, and as Mr. Barnham drew her gently towards the nearest sofa he felt as if she was nothing more than a child he must comfort.

He helped Romana to sit down and found as she was holding onto him with her head on his shoulder he was forced to sit with her, his arm still round her.

"Now, what is all this about?" he asked in a quiet, kind voice. "You have been so brave and sensible up until now. What has upset you?"

"It is . . that m . man," Romana sobbed. "H . he said . . that Nicole . . Nicole . . whom I love . . is a . . pros . . prosti . . tute!"

Her voice broke on the words so that they were almost incoherent, and she cried even more violently than she had done before.

Mr. Barnham looked at the Marquis as if for an explanation.

"I was trying to get the truth out of her," the Marquis said in a somewhat embarrassed voice. "I thought we should have to face facts sooner or later."

Mr. Barnham did not express his disapproval in words, but he certainly looked at his employer in a manner which said quite clearly that he thought the Marquis had been unwise and certainly inconsiderate.

Romana's tears were abating a little and after a moment Mr. Barnham said:

"Suppose we talk about this quietly? Just between the three of us?"

"I . . I want to g . go away," Romana said. "I want to . . go home. Please, give me enough money to go home. Then you . . need never . . s . see me again."

"I am afraid that is not possible," Mr. Barnham answered. "I am sure later, when things are not as difficult as they are now, you will be able to go back to see your friends, if that is what you want."

"I . . want to get . . away," Romana said in a whisper.

"I can understand that," Mr. Barnham answered. "This has been a great shock for you as it has been for the Marquis too. You have to think of him as well as yourself."

"Why should I do . . that?" Romana enquired with her face hidden against Mr. Barnham's shoulder. "He is . . horrible . . he . . tells lies . . cruel lies! . . he is bad . . wicked . . and . . I will not . . stay with . . him!"

Mr. Barnham could not help thinking with just a touch of amusement that it was unlikely the Marquis had ever in his whole life, heard himself described in such terms, but aloud he said:

"I think perhaps you are being a little unjust. Will you try to stop crying, then I will explain things to you, and perhaps you can explain certain things to us which we do not understand."

"What . . sort of . . things?"

"Shall we start by talking about your friend, Nicole de Prêt? You sound as if you know her well, and I would like to hear about her."

There was a distinct pause and Mr. Barnham knew that Romana was fighting for self-control. Then she said in a very small voice:

"I . . I will . . try."

She started to raise her head from his shoulder, then realising she had no handkerchief, put her fingers up to her wet cheeks.

Mr. Barnham's free hand went to his pocket only to find that he too was without a handkerchief and he looked at the Marquis with a faint smile.

His Lordship produced a square of the finest linen and handed it to his secretary.

"Wipe your eyes," Mr. Barnham said gently, "and

perhaps you would like a drink?"

"I . . would like some . . water," Romana said, "if it is . . no trouble."

The Marquis walked across the room to where there was a grog-tray in one corner.

He brought back a heavily cut crystal glass filled with cold water and Mr. Barnham put it into Romana's hand.

She took several small sips, then he took the glass from her and put it down on a side-table.

She had wiped her cheeks, but her lashes were still wet and dark, and he thought she was one of the few women who could cry without having swollen eyes or looking somehow disfigured.

He took his arm from Romana and glanced at the Marquis who, as if he knew what was expected of him, sat down in a chair facing them.

"Now," Mr. Barnham said. "Suppose we start from the very beginning of this unhappy story? Will you tell us first about your friend Nicole?"

"Nicole has . . always been my . . friend," Romana said. "When the Comte and Comtesse de Prêt escaped from France during the Revolution their son was guillotined . . but they brought . . Nicole to England . . with them."

She caught her breath for a moment before she went on:

"They had very little money, although the Comte had been a very rich man when they lived in France. In fact, all they had was the jewellery which the Comtesse was wearing and they sold that bit by bit, until there was no more left to sell."

Both the Marquis and Mr. Barnham were listening intently as she went on:

"It was . . then that Nicole . . decided she would go to London and try to earn some . . money from her . . dancing. She had heard there were Dancing Schools and she . . thought she would be a . . teacher."

Romana glanced defiantly at the Marquis as if she dared him to contradict her.

"She obtained a position as a teacher in a Dancing-School near Covent Garden and she was so . . successful that soon she was . . sending home quite a lot of . . money to

83

her father and mother."

As if he was afraid, the Marquis might say something disparaging, Mr. Barnham said quickly:

"I understand. And you thought as you needed money too you would join your friend."

"Nicole is older than I am, but we have always done . . everything together. She is like my . . sister."

Romana looked straight at the Marquis and added:

"She was sweet and gentle . . and very, very . . good. She would never do . . anything wrong or . . wicked."

"Then why was she with Kirkhampton?" the Marquis asked, almost as if he was goaded into a reply.

"How can Her Ladyship know that, if she only arrived in London that evening?" Mr. Barnham enquired.

"That . . terrible man must have . . somehow got Nicole into his . . clutches," Romana said. "She could not like him . . she could not! I knew she was upset when he said I had to . . marry the . . man who was . . unconscious in the . . chair."

Her voice broke again as she said:

"Nicole was . . crying and she told me there was . . nothing she could . . do to . . prevent it."

The Marquis was just about to say that Nicole de Prêt might have refused to invite him to supper in the first place, when he met Mr. Barnham's eyes and bit back the words before they passed his lips.

"I do not . . understand why Nicole . . behaved the way she did," Romana went on, "except that she was frightened and Lord Kirkhampton must have been . . threatening her as he . . threatened me. But why should he have . . wished for . . you to be . . married anyway?"

"Because he hates me and wishes to injure me," the Marquis answered.

"But I had never seen you before," Romana said, "so why should he force me to marry you?"

The Marquis thought that doubtless Kirkhampton at the last moment, had turned back from actually murdering him because the appearance of Romana in her old-fashioned country-clothes must have seemed a better way of getting his revenge without actually committing a crime for which he could be arrested.

He thought Mr. Barnham was thinking the same thing because after a moment his secretary said:

"Now we understand Your Ladyship's part in this unpleasant episode. I am sure His Lordship regrets anything he might have said to hurt or upset you."

Romana did not reply. Mr. Barnham could still feel her resentment, and after a moment he said:

"Suppose you look at it for a moment not from your point of view, which I admit is a very upsetting one, but from that of the man you were forced to marry?"

He knew that Romana was listening and went on:

"The Marquis, although you have seen him in very different circumstances, is usually a very charming person, a great sportsman, and has a position of social importance that makes him a distinguished figure in every walk of life."

There was a faint smile on Mr. Barnham's lips as he continued:

"You will understand that there have been a great many ladies, and very beautiful ones over many years, who have wished to marry His Lordship."

He knew Romana gave a little shudder, since the idea of marriage to him was repulsive to her, but he went on:

"The Marquis has been waiting, perhaps romantically, until he would meet the person who he thought was right for him, and with whom he would fall in love."

Romana raised her eyes to his as if doubting what he said.

"I am sure," Mr. Barnham continued, "that you have felt the same. You too wanted to be in love with the man you married."

"Yes . . of course," Romana said in a low voice.

"Then you will understand that if this is a shock for you, it is equally a shock for the Marquis," Mr. Barnham said. "He is now twenty-eight, and although he wished to marry sometime, he was waiting until he could find someone who would be worthy not only of being the chatelaine of Sarne and his other houses, but would also bear his name with distinction and be a credit to his family which has been part of the history of England for over five hundred years."

Romana drew in her breath and Mr. Barnham said:

"You can therefore, understand that to come round from a state of unconsciousness and find himself saddled with a wife, he has never seen before and about whom he knows nothing, except that she was chosen for him by his bitterest enemy, would be a shock to any man!"

He paused before he added:

"But perhaps especially to the Marquis, who like the Prince in the fairy-story had been always looking for the woman of his dreams."

Mr. Barnham thought to himself mockingly that he was becoming very lyrical.

At the same time, he was sure that from what he had seen of Romana she was not only sensitive and vulnerable, but also idealistic.

He had studied her very carefully all the while they had been travelling from London, and he had admired her self-control and the way she had not complained or ranted against fate, but behaved in what he told himself was an extremely well-bred and civilised manner.

He thought too, that at this moment she was being very restrained.

While he was aware that she was tense and her tears were not far from the surface, there was something dignified in the manner in which she was listening to him and trying to understand what he was saying.

"What I want you both to try to do now," Mr. Barnham said, "is to appreciate not only your own difficulties, but each other's."

He looked at the Marquis before he added:

"I am sure, My Lord, you did not realise the affection Her Ladyship has for Nicole de Prêt, or that they were brought up together before you accused her of things which I am quite certain are untrue."

The Marquis could not fail to understand what Mr. Barnham expected of him, and with an effort he said:

"I must apologise if I was mistaken in what I thought."

"You *were* mistaken," Romana said positively. "I am sure of it, and now that you understand that I was not willingly involved in the . . plot to marry you and have no wish to be your wife, I would . . like to . . leave."

"Now that is something I must explain to you," Mr. Barnham said quickly before the Marquis could speak, "and I want you to try to understand what I am saying."

"I will . . try," Romana said.

"Lord Kirkhampton is a very revengeful man and a bad loser," Mr. Barnham began. "He hates the Marquis mostly because he is more successful on the race-course than he is. He is out to injure His Lordship in every possible way he can, and you have seen the evidence of what he has done already."

"Yes . . but I do not . . see why that means I must . . stay here."

"I am afraid that is just what it does mean," Mr. Barnham replied. "You see, if you leave the Marquis so soon after your marriage, then Lord Kirkhampton would start a scandal and would also undoubtedly follow you wherever you went and try to make trouble, both for you and the husband you have left behind."

"Could he . . really do that?" Romana asked.

"I assure you that is what he will do," Mr. Barnham said.

"He does not . . sound as if he is quite . . sane."

"Perhaps he is not," Mr. Barnham agreed. "People who are obsessed with hatred are, in my opinion, not normal."

"Then . . I have to . . stay here?"

"For the time being," Mr. Barnham said, "and may I suggest that instead of quarrelling and making yourselves more unhappy you try to make the best of things. Perhaps we will be able to find a solution, I do not know. But for the moment, if you behave with propriety in public and a friendly fashion in private, perhaps it will not be as difficult as you both anticipate."

He knew as he spoke, that for the first time in their unusual acquaintance with each other, the Marquis was thinking of Romana, and Romana of the Marquis.

She was looking at him tentatively from under her wet eye-lashes, and after a moment she said:

"I will . . try to do what you want . . I am sorry I . . cried."

"I am sure you could not help it," Mr. Barnham said. "As I have already said, you have been extremely brave up until now."

He rose to his feet.

"I came to tell you, My Lord, that there is a groom here with a message from Lord Lovell asking if you could possibly see him tomorrow about something which concerns the boundary of your two estates. His Lordship very much regrets asking such a thing when you are on your honeymoon, but he promises he will not occupy your time for more than half-an-hour."

"Yes, of course. Tell His Lordship that I shall be pleased to see him at whatever time suits him," the Marquis replied.

Mr. Barnham bowed and left the room.

The door closed behind him and there was a silence in which both the Marquis and Romana sat not looking at each other, but very conscious that they were alone together.

Then the Marquis, as if with an effort, said:

"I think Barnham has cleared things up between us. I will try, Romana, to be more pleasant than I have been up-to-date."

"Thank . . you."

"As Barnham said, you have been very brave and I realised tonight you were trying to put a good face on things in front of the servants. I will be more helpful on future occasions."

He put out his hand towards her, then realised there was an obvious hesitation before she put hers into his, and as their fingers touched, he knew incredibly that she was still afraid.

He had meant to kiss her hand as if to seal the pact between them, but he was aware that it would upset her again so after a moment he released her hand and walked across the room to the grog-tray.

As he poured himself a drink it struck him that never in his whole long and passionate acquaintance with women, who had loved him desperately had there ever been one who was actually afraid of him.

.　.　.　.　.

The Marquis drew in his horse and Romana did the same.

"I brought you here," he said, "because it is believed

88

that on a clear day, one can see for fifty miles. I doubt it, but it makes a good story for the country folk to tell.".

Romana laughed.

"They always have stories which they repeat and repeat until they believe them themselves."

"You will find Sarne is full of them," the Marquis said. "There is a tree which if you stand under it at a full moon makes you fall in love with the next person you meet; and there is a wishing-well in the garden that, I am told, is infallible, except that one's wishes, when they do come true, are not always exactly what one expected."

Romana laughed again.

"That is true, I am sure, of all wishes, and of all prayers."

"Of prayers?" the Marquis questioned.

"Mama always advised me when I prayed for something I particularly wanted to add at the end when I spoke to God: 'if You think best'. She always said that God knows better than we do what is good for us."

"I suppose that is true," the Marquis said reflectively. "I have never thought of it before."

He actually thought it was a long time since God had been introduced into any conversation that he had with a woman, but then he had been finding out in the last two days that Romana was quite different from any woman he had known before.

He still resented the fact that he was married to her. He still found it hard at times, to believe that she really was what she appeared to be.

He could not help waiting almost instinctively for the moment when she showed herself up in her true colours, and he would learn that indeed she was nothing but a scheming tool for Kirkhampton and a willing agent in the revenge he had planned.

And yet in the last two days, when he had shown her Sarne and they had ridden together and driven to the farms for her to meet some of the more important employees on the estate, he had found that she behaved in a manner that he could not fault however hard he tried.

As if he did not wish to probe too deeply into matters which upset her, he refrained from asking her questions about herself or indeed about Nicole de Prêt.

Not for one moment was he deceived into thinking that Nicole was anything except what he thought her to be, a high-class, expensive prostitute or, if the word sounded better, a cocotte; but he was now almost prepared to believe that Romana did not know this and did in fact, think her the pure and innocent girl with whom she had played since childhood.

And at the same time, something cynical in the Marquis did not allow him to accept the whole story without reservation.

How could it be possible for any girl of her age, if she was from a decent family and as refined as she pretended to be, to travel alone to London without even a maid?

Then to stay alone with another girl, apparently unchaperoned, and to have been credulous enough to think that a teacher in a school of dancing, if there were such places, could make enough money to keep her father and mother in comfort.

He was very sceptical as to whether the Comte and Comtesse really existed, or, if they did, whether their title was genuine.

Any number of émigrés from France had arrived in England, giving themselves aristocratic backgrounds to which they were certainly not entitled.

The Marquis determined that on his return to London he would seek out some of the real French aristocrats who had not yet returned to France, as they had been invited to do by Napoleon Bonaparte and discover if the family of de Prêt really existed.

At the same time, he told himself that whatever he discovered, whatever he learnt about Nicole de Prêt would not in any way, affect his marriage to Romana.

That was a *fait accompli* which nothing could alter, but at the same time, he was beginning to think that things might have been very much worse and perhaps in some way in which he could not envisage, he might have the laugh on Kirkhampton.

He told himself that Barnham, who had been completely and absolutely beguiled by Romana and believed every word she said, was not such an astute or such a suspicious judge of character as he was.

She might be everything she pretended to be, young, innocent, a lady by birth, but there was still some critical part of his brain that would not capitulate so easily.

He found however, that she was definitely intelligent, although he was not anxious to spend more time in talking to her than was absolutely necessary.

He had busied himself for the last two days in the affairs of the estate, and although for appearance's sake he rode with Romana and took her driving and inevitably they were together at meal-times, it was easy to contrive that there were not long hours spent in each other's company, when he might be doing something else.

He had discovered that she rode well and was, as he would have expected, delighted with his horses.

It was now only the second morning that they had ridden together when he thought that in the summer habit of hyacinth blue which had 'Bond Street' stamped all over it, she looked surprisingly attractive.

She had, he thought, some of the grace and sensitivity that had attracted him to Nicole de Prêt, and she had too, which he had only discovered that morning, a spontaneous, joyous little laugh, which had something very young about it.

The Marquis was used to women laughing at what he said because he was considered a wit, but their laughter was usually deliberately musical and often deliberately contrived.

With Romana it was clearly spontaneous, a sound as fresh as the wind in the trees or water rising from a fountain.

He knew when she laughed that she forgot her fear of him.

Nevertheless, he found himself looking for that little flicker in her eyes if he came too near to her, or which appeared when he said something more firmly or violently than if he spoke indifferently.

"It is lovely!" Romana said, looking at the view.

He knew that for the moment she had forgotten him as a

man and was not acutely conscious of him as any other woman he was riding with would have been.

She was tracing the turns in the river with her eyes. Then she said:

"I suppose, if one was high up in the sky, above the world, all the land would like that."

"Like what?" he asked.

"Like a map," she said.

"Yes, of course," he agreed, "but that is one way we will never see it."

"Unless of course we went up in a balloon."

"I had forgotten about balloons," the Marquis said, "but personally I have no wish to fly in one."

"I think it would be exciting," Romana said. "I read Papa the description of the balloon which went up from Vauxhall Gardens. We both thought it would be a new and thrilling way of seeing the world."

"It is easy to go up in a balloon," the Marquis said, "but much more difficult to come safely down again."

"I suppose that also applies to people," Romana said. "They become inflated with their own success and are never again nice and ordinary as they were before it all happened."

"You sound disillusioned," the Marquis smiled, "or is it cynical?"

"I hope I am neither," Romana answered, "but of course, I know very few people who have been successful, while you must have known hundreds."

"Quite a lot," the Marquis agreed.

He was just going to say: "I wonder what you will think of my friends?" but instead he found himself asking what his friends would think about her.

Would they be suspicious of her? he asked himself.

He was certainly not as afraid of their meeting her as he had been at first.

Even now he could remember how ghastly she had looked with a great red mark on her face, the crumpled, old-fashioned skirts lying around her and her bonnet knocked sideways on her head.

He had thought then that he would rather die than introduce such a woman as his wife, but now if Romana always behaved as she had been doing this last forty-eight hours, there was really nothing to worry about.

And yet he was not sure.

Could she be putting on a very clever act? Could Kirkhampton have tutored her until she was almost word-perfect? Then when he was beguiled into a false sense of security would he spring some terrible and horrible scandal upon him which would defame not only himself but the name he bore?

The Marquis without even being aware of it, was looking at Romana's profile as she stared out over the countryside below them.

Then as if she could feel his doubts and fears vibrating towards her, she turned her head and looked at him.

"What . . what are you . . thinking?" she asked.

"I am trying to understand you," he said.

"Why? Why should you . . want to do . . that?"

"Why not? And why should you be afraid of my doing so?"

It was a pertinent question and he wondered if she would answer it.

Then suddenly the fear was back in her eyes and without replying she turned her horse round sharply.

To the Marquis's surprise she was riding ahead of him down the hill, back the way they had come.

When she reached flatter land she was galloping violently in a manner that made it impossible for him to catch up with her until they were within sight of Sarne.

CHAPTER FIVE

"She is charming, absolutely charming!" Lady Lovell said. "You must tell me, Vallient, where you met her, and why we have never heard of her before."

The Marquis thought that Lady Lovell, who had known him ever since he was a child, had always been a bore. He disliked her over-enthusiastic manner of talking and the way once she got onto a subject she worried at it, like a dog with a bone.

He was, in fact, wondering what Romana was saying to the Lord Chief Justice at the other end of the table.

When Lord Lovell had called on him the previous morning to discuss some difficulty over the common boundary of their estates, he had said before he left:

"I am sure you will not wish to break your tradition of giving a luncheon, as you always have, for the Lord Chief Justice? He is staying with us tomorrow night, and I know he is looking forward to coming to Sarne again."

It was an annual arrangement that the Marquis had forgotten and he knew now, even with the excuse of being on his honeymoon, that it would be rude to refuse an old man who had been a friend of himself and his family ever since he could remember.

"Of course," he answered, "I shall be delighted to welcome the Lord Chief Justice, with yourself and Lady Lovell, and of course the whole entourage, as I always have."

Lord Lovell had laughed.

"I am afraid that will make it twelve of us, since His Lordship, as you know, travels in style. But I can reassure you by saying that his private Chaplain is a much more

94

pleasant man than we had to endure last year."

"That is undoubtedly a relief," the Marquis remarked.

As soon as Lord Lovell had left he had sent for Mr. Barnham to tell him there would be a luncheon-party the following day.

Although neither of the men mentioned it to each other, they were both wondering how Romana would react to her first social occasion, and a rather important one.

Lord Lovell was Lord Lieutenant of the County and he had already announced that he wished to retire in a year's time. It was obvious that he would recommend to the King that the Marquis should take his place.

As a Lord Lieutenant officially representing His Majesty, it was absolutely essential that his wife should be everything that was desirable from the Court point of view.

Mr. Barnham was well aware of this, and he had several times in the last few years been apprehensive that the Marquis might marry somebody who would not be able to take up the position that was required of her.

It was not so important in London, in the raffish society that surrounded the Prince of Wales, but in the country propriety and dignity were essential.

The Marquis did not express his fears, but when he was alone Mr. Barnham reassured himself that Romana would do everything that was expected of her.

At the same time he was well aware the following morning that his employer was nervous.

Looking down the table now over the profusion of priceless gold ornaments, set between the Sèvres dishes which held the huge peaches and muscat grapes that were grown in the greenhouses at Sarne, the Marquis wondered what on earth Romana could be saying to the Lord Chief Justice.

It was obvious that the old man, an extremely distinguished figure and good-looking even for his age, was listening to her intently, and the Marquis had not missed the fact that he had made no effort to address one word to his Chaplain, who was sitting on his other side.

It was in fact an all male party with the exception of Lady Lovell and Romana.

Lord Lovell was on Romana's left and he thought she should have spoken to him or at least drawn him into the conversation with the Lord Chief Justice.

He suddenly had the horrible fear that she was taking him into her confidence and asking him if it was possible to break a marriage which had taken place in such unhappy circumstances.

Then he told himself she would not do anything so reprehensible or, from his point of view, scandalous. And yet he was not sure. What else could they be discussing so fervently? he wondered and found it hard to bring his mind back to Lady Lovell.

"We have been longing for you to get married for so long, Vallient," she was saying. "After all, it is not only important for you personally to have a wife, but it means so much to Sarne and, for that matter, the County."

She waited for the Marquis to agree with her and as he did not speak, went on:

"As soon as your honeymoon is over I shall come and talk to your wife and persuade her to help me with so many charities and organisations that are sadly lacking in new blood and new ideas."

She paused to look down the table at Romana who still was talking with noticeable animation to the Lord Chief Justice. Then she said:

"How pleased your dear mother would be to know that you are married and not to one of those fast and fashionable young women from London, about whom we have heard such hair-raising tales."

The Marquis thought that Lady Lovell was presuming too much on her long acquaintance by speaking in a manner which he would not have tolerated from anyone who was not old enough to be his mother.

"You should not believe everything you hear," he remarked scathingly.

"I try not to," Lady Lovell replied with a smile, "and of course I understand, dear Vallient that because you are so attractive and so well endowed with this world's goods, it is impossible for people not to gossip about you. At the same time . . ."

Then, as if it suddenly percolated her rather stupid mind that the Marquis was annoyed, she checked what she had been about to say and merely added:

"I am so happy, so very happy about your marriage to such a nice girl."

The Marquis could not help wondering what Lady Lovell would say if she knew the circumstances in which he and what she called "a nice girl" had been married.

The fact that he had been unconscious in the house of a prostitute would hardly be Lady Lovell's idea of a good way to start off his married life.

He looked down the table again at Romana and felt all his resentment at what had happened surge over him in a wave of fury.

Lady Lovell might say he had been gossiped about and he was well aware of it, but he had always taken care that he did not outrage the proprieties or lay himself open to be criticised unnecessarily.

He had always been particularly careful when he was in the country, which was why he never invited his more raffish friends to Sarne.

Unlike the practice of other noblemen, the women who embellished his shooting-parties in the winter or his racing-parties in the spring were always acceptable members of the *Beau Monde*.

It was all the more infuriating therefore that he should be suspicious that his wife was by no means the innocent girl she appeared to be, and he could not help wondering how soon it would be before some of her lovers appeared.

He was quite certain he would realise what they were by the look in their eyes even before any innuendos in what they said made him aware of the truth.

The Marquis shrank from the thought of finding himself in such a situation, and since he had found himself married to Romana he had often thought as he walked up the stairs or along the corridors that the eyes of his ancestors in their gilt-framed portraits looked at him with contempt.

They had managed to avoid such a major catastrophe, though he knew that a large number of them had behaved in what today would have been considered an outrageous fashion.

Yet they had never brought bad blood into the family. Not even the Sarne who had been notorious for his love-affairs in the reign of Charles II had been foolish enough as to marry one of the loose women in whom the Court abounded.

Instead he had chosen the highly respectable, if somewhat plainer daughter of a neighbouring Duke and left her in the country while he lived a riotous life at Whitehall.

It struck the Marquis as he looked at the handsome, but dissolute face of this ancestor that that was what he himself had intended to do in the future.

His wife, like many of the previous chatelaines of Sarne, would stay here with their children while he, when it suited him, would go a-roaming on his own.

Yet even that pleasure was now denied him and he knew that Mr. Barnham was right when he said that for the moment at any rate he and Romana must be together, to prevent Lord Kirkhampton from making a scandal out of their being apart.

'It is intolerable!' the Marquis thought.

But if he was honest he had not found it boring to ride with Romana, and last night at dinner when she had not been so nervous or so frightened of him, as she had been at first, they had had quite an interesting conversation.

Looking back the Marquis realised that she had not said very much, but she had drawn him out on the subject of his horses and they talked in a different manner from the previous evening.

He thought unless it was an act, she had seemed really interested in the reasons why his horses had won so many of the Classic races in the last few years.

He wondered now if she was speaking to the Lord Chief Justice about racing, but thought it unlikely.

He could never remember His Lordship showing any interest in the 'sport of Kings'. In fact on his previous visits to Sarne he had thought him somewhat of a bore unless the conversation was on legal matters, which tended to narrow the field of discussion.

Romana and the Lord Chief Justice were still talking,

and the Marquis felt his anger rising.

He was sure now she was being indiscreet and he wondered how he could possibly prevent her from saying more than she had already, then knew it was impossible.

"As soon as you have finished your honeymoon, Vallient," Lady Lovell said beside him, "I will give a party to introduce your wife to our neighbours. You can imagine how curious they are! In fact, your marriage was a shock for us all. But why did you have to be so precipitate, so that none of us had time to send you a present?"

"As you must have read in *'The Gazette',* my wife is in mourning," the Marquis replied, knowing she was waiting for an answer.

"Yes, I read that," Lady Lovell replied, "but it told me so little. Was it her father or her mother who had died?"

"Her father."

"And who was he?"

The Marquis realised somewhat belatedly that neither he nor Mr. Barnham had thought out an answer to this sort of question.

"His name was Wardell," he replied, smiling so as to take the abruptness from his tone.

"I am aware of that, stupid boy!" Lady Lovell laughed, "but tell me about him. Where did he live? My husband was saying that he knew some Wardells who lived in Leicestershire."

"Romana's parents lived in Northumberland," the Marquis replied.

He thought as he spoke, that was the sum total of his knowledge where Romana was concerned and cursed himself, or rather Mr. Barnham, for not having acquired or invented more details.

He was well aware now that Lady Lovell's curiosity would be echoed by dozens of other women once he began to meet them.

It was inconceivable that he, the Marquis of Sarne, would marry a nobody, and he thought savagely that Mr. Barnham and he would have to sit down and invent a whole family history to make his marriage to Romana sound credible from a social point of view.

'I can hardly tell the truth,' he thought bitterly.

He pictured Romana as he had first seen her lying on the floor with the imprint of Lord Kirkhampton's hand on her cheek . . .

He realised with a sense of relief that luncheon was coming to an end, and he hoped that Romana would realise it and rise to her feet.

"Dammit," he muttered beneath his breath, "she does not know how to behave properly."

"What was the name of your wife's mother before she married?" Lady Lovell had just asked.

As she spoke, Romana rose reluctantly, still having a last word as she did so with the Lord Chief Justice.

She looked at Lady Lovell who also rose.

"Never mind," she said to the Marquis as if he was about to reply, "I am sure your wife will tell me all I want to know. At the same time, do not leave it too long before you join us. It is so bad for Lovell to drink port, but he can never resist it!"

She walked from the Marquis's side as she spoke and joined Romana who was waiting for her at the door.

As the two ladies left the men sat down again, except that the Lord Chief Justice walked to the end of the table to seat himself next to the Marquis in the chair vacated by Lady Lovell.

As he did so, he said:

"I congratulate you, Sarne, and that is no figure of speech. It has been a pleasure I cannot describe to meet Arnold Wardell's daughter and find that she is married to you."

With some difficulty the Marquis managed to exclaim:

"You knew my wife's father?"

"Very well indeed!" the Lord Chief Justice replied, "in fact our friendship was one of which I am extremely proud."

The Marquis hoped he did not show the surprise he was feeling as the Lord Chief Justice continued:

"If ever there was a man who deserved recognition not only in this country, but from the world, it was Arnold Wardell. But of course he was very retiring, and I suppose the war was instrumental in preventing him from being approached as he should have been."

"In what way?" the Marquis asked.

"My dear boy, when there is a man of Wardell's ability, it is a disgrace—an absolute disgrace—that he should not have been recognised in an appropriate manner. But instead, your wife tells me, he has for years been ignored and obviously forgotten."

The Marquis chose his words with care, not wishing to seem as ignorant as he actually was.

"Why do you think he deserved such recognition, My Lord?"

"Why?" the Lord Chief Justice enquired. "Because there is no Greek scholar in my estimation in any other nation who can hold a candle to Wardell. His translations of Sophocles' plays are streets beyond those of any other scholar, and his poems of Pindar were so magnificent that I consider for them alone, he should have been given a Knighthood."

The Marquis did not speak and the Lord Chief Justice went on:

"I blame myself for not speaking of him to the Prime Minister, but as I say, the war made us forget many other things of importance, including culture, and authors, as you are well aware, have never received their rightful recognition or been properly appreciated in this country."

This was obviously a favourite hobby-horse of the Lord Chief Justice, and he went on deprecating the fact that the British as a whole were an uncultured race who had never encouraged or rewarded their men of letters, but the Marquis was wracking his brains.

He thought now that he must have heard of Arnold Wardell.

He was sure that when he was at Oxford his books had been part of the curriculum of the classical languages which he had studied.

Greek had not been of any particular interest to him after he left the University, but he was aware that if the Lord Chief Justice was impressed by Romana's father, then other people would feel the same.

The Lord Chief Justice was still talking about his friend, then he said with a faint smile:

"I have admired you as a sportsman, Sarne, but I shall now look forward to admiring your intellect. No-one could marry Arnold Wardell's daughter without having a strong conception of the influence Greek philosophy and Greek thinking has had on the development of mankind. I had never suspected in the past that you were interested in such things. I feel now that I should apologise to you for my stupidity."

"I hope you will do nothing of the sort," the Marquis said quickly.

"Your wife tells me that she has worked with her father ever since her mother died. I am hoping that she will be able to finish some of his current work which he was unable to complete himself. You must encourage her, Sarne. The world cannot afford to lose a genius like Wardell or the inheritance that he has left us."

The Marquis, who was not certain what he should reply, smiled and the Lord Chief Justice put out his hand to lay it on his arm.

"You are young," he said, "and like all young people you are concerned only with today and the enjoyment it brings. Promise me that you will encourage your wife to complete her father's work. It is important, desperately important to the future of those who seek knowledge."

The Lord Chief Justice was speaking so intently that the Marquis could only say:

"Of course, My Lord, if you ask it of me, I will do everything in my power to help Romana as you suggest."

"Thank you," the Lord Chief Justice said, "and if she succeeds, as I have a feeling she is well qualified to do, then untold generations in the future will thank you too."

Astounded but feeling that if this conversation continued he might put his foot in it, the Marquis rose, and the other gentlemen followed him and the Lord Chief Justice into the Salon where Lady Lovell and Romana were waiting for them.

As the Lord Chief Justice had to be on his way, there was only time to say good-bye and thank the Marquis for an excellent luncheon.

"Do not forget your promise, my boy," he said as the

Marquis walked with him to the front door.

Lady Lovell was more effusive.

"Your wife is sweet, and I am so happy for you, dear Vallient," she said. "How clever, how very clever of you to find someone so perfect, not only for yourself but for Sarne."

As the three carriages in which his guests had arrived drove away, the Marquis stood looking after them, a somewhat bewildered expression on his face.

He found that Romana was not beside him on the steps but had gone back to the Salon.

She was reading a newspaper as he entered the room, but she put it down quickly as if she was afraid he would not expect her to be concerned with such things.

As he walked towards her he thought that once again she was looking afraid.

"I am . . sorry," she said, as the Marquis reached her side.

"For what?" he enquired.

"I know you are going to tell me that I talked to the Lord Chief Justice too much and not enough to Lord Lovell, but it was difficult."

"I understand he knew your father."

"Yes, and he said such very kind and wonderful things about Papa. It is a long time since I have had a really intelligent conversation with anyone."

She spoke without thinking, then stopped and looked apprehensively at the Marquis.

"I am . . sorry," she said again.

The Marquis laughed.

"You are certainly very frank, Romana! I realise now I have heard about your father that I have been extremely remiss in not finding out more about you before. Why did you not tell me who he was?"

"I did not think that you would be . . interested, or that it would . . mean anything to you."

The Marquis smiled a little wryly.

It was quite obvious that Romana had not a very high opinion of his intelligence.

"As it happens," he said, "I studied Greek at Oxford. I

am sure, therefore, that I have read one or more of your father's books."

"You have?" Romana exclaimed, and now there was no mistaking the delight in her voice.

"It was a long time ago," the Marquis said, "and I am sure that now I am rather rusty, but I dare say what I learnt would come back to me."

"Of course it will," Romana said. "It is something you never forget, and Papa's books are of course, in English. Unfortunately there are none in your Library."

"You have looked?" the Marquis asked.

"Yes, of course," she replied, "I wanted to read them myself."

"Then we will send for copies."

"I have one he had not finished with me," Romana said, "but perhaps that would not interest you."

"It would interest me very much," the Marquis replied, "although I have a feeling I shall not be able to help you, as the Lord Chief Justice suggested, in finishing your father's book."

"I should like you to try."

She spoke impulsively, then she hesitated.

". . unless, of course, it would . . bore you."

"You have made it very clear what you think of my intellectual ability," the Marquis said, "but just as I have been surprised by what I have learnt about you, perhaps I shall be able to surprise you about myself."

"I am . . sure you . . will."

"You can show me what you have with you tonight," the Marquis said, "but may I suggest that for what is left of the afternoon we go for a drive? I have arranged to visit one of the farms on the East side of the estate. But, if you wish, we can postpone it."

"No, of course not," Romana said quickly. "We must not waste the sunshine. It may rain tomorrow."

"In which case," the Marquis said, "I shall undoubtedly spend the day swatting at my Greek before you can have a chance to tell me how ignorant I am."

"I would be much too frightened to do that," Romana said.

She spoke lightly, but the Marquis had an idea that this was another way in which he could frighten her.

When they returned from their drive Mr. Barnham was waiting for them with the letters which had been brought down from Sarne House in London by a groom.

"Congratulations are pouring in, My Lord," he said, "and already over fifty parcels have arrived containing presents."

The Marquis groaned.

"Does that mean I shall have to write and thank for them?"

"I am afraid so," Mr. Barnham replied, "but to make it easier I will acknowledge their arrival, then you can write at your leisure."

"Perhaps I can help you," Romana suggested impulsively.

The Marquis raised his eye-brows, then he said:

"Why not? After all, the presents are for the bride and the bridegroom. Except for near relations and very close friends, people will be just as pleased to have a letter from you as from me."

"I always wrote all Papa's letters for him," Romana said, "and so I am quite happy to do yours."

"I shall be extremely grateful," the Marquis replied. "If there is one thing I really loathe it is having to write letters."

"With the result," Mr. Barnham smiled, "that they are short and very much to the point."

"I will do all the ones that have to be fulsome," Romana promised.

"I am sure you will do it exceedingly well," the Marquis said, and added:

"You have not heard, Barnham, what I have just discovered about Her Ladyship."

"What is that?" Mr. Barnham asked.

The Marquis told him what the Lord Chief Justice had said.

"But of course!" Mr. Barnham exclaimed. "I have been wondering all the time why the name Wardell rang a bell, but it never struck me for one moment that Arnold Wardell might be a relation, let alone your father."

Romana gave a little smile.

"I suppose I must look so stupid," she said, "that no-one expects me to have such a brilliant and clever father. It is rather unfair."

Mr. Barnham thought she looked very young and lovely and it was therefore unlikely that anyone would expect her to be clever too.

He knew that nothing could be better or more encouraging to the Marquis than to find that his wife was not the nonentity he had thought her to be but, from a scholar's point of view, very important indeed.

"I remember some of the poems your father translated," he said aloud to Romana, "and I thought they were absolutely beautiful."

"I love them too," Romana said, "I learnt some of them when I was little and when I helped him translate them I realised how brilliant he was in being able to express the fundamental meaning of the author in English, when some of the Greek words seemed to me to be untranslatable."

"I always thought that must be so," Mr. Barnham agreed. "Greek thoughts are deep so that ordinary mundane vocabulary is quite inadequate to express the depth and breadth of what they were trying to say."

"You understand!" Romana said with a little sigh.

"I want to understand too," the Marquis said as if he felt he was being left out. "That is why tonight you must bring down your father's work that you have with you, and we will try to work on it together."

"I am only . . afraid it might . . bore you."

"If I am bored I shall say so," the Marquis replied, "but I have a feeling that I am going to find it absorbingly interesting."

"I am sorry to upset your plans," Mr. Barnham interposed, "but one reason why I wished to see you, My Lord, was to tell you that on Thursday Mr. Evan Stanley is selling fifty of his best horses."

"Good God!" the Marquis ejaculated. "Why was I not told this before?"

"I am afraid, My Lord, the letter was delayed in reaching

106

Sarne House and had been there for two days before it arrived here this morning."

"I told Stanley I was interested in at least half-a-dozen of his race horses, and in his brood mare."

"Yes, I know, My Lord, and he wrote to you personally. But, as I say, the letter was delayed."

"You say the sale is on Thursday?"

"Yes, My Lord. He says in his letter that you shall have the pick before they are put up for auction."

"There is hardly time for me to do that," the Marquis said in an irritated tone. "Or have you any suggestions?"

"I was thinking," Mr. Barnham replied, "that the best thing would be for you and Her Ladyship to go to London tomorrow. Your Lordship could either stay at Sarne House or, alternatively, journey back to Baldock where Mr. Stanley has his stables and stay the night, as you have done before, at '*The Green Dragon*'."

"Yes, of course. I will do that," the Marquis agreed, "and that would mean I could see the horses first thing in the morning before the sale starts."

He paused a moment before he said:

"I want to watch his race-horses on the gallops. There are three I am certain I wish to include in my own stable. The others are unknown to me."

"That would be a very good arrangement," Mr. Barnham said, "and if you return to London immediately after the sale, Her Ladyship need only spend one night alone at Sarne House."

"I do not wish to be a .. bother to you," Romana said. "I will stay here .. if you .. prefer."

Mr. Barnham looked at the Marquis and they were both thinking about Lord Kirkhampton.

"I think it would be best if you went with His Lordship," Mr. Barnham said. "As it happens I am sure you could spend the time shopping. Mrs. Hughes has already informed me there are quite a number of things that are urgently required in your trousseau."

Romana laughed.

"I cannot think what they can be. I have never had so many beautiful clothes. In fact I can never make up my mind which to wear next."

"I am sure that Mrs. Hughes will be only too willing to prepare a list," Mr. Barnham said with a smile.

"Then I will take Mrs. Mayfield shopping with me," Romana said, "but I am afraid it will be an expensive expedition."

"I doubt if you will spend as much as His Lordship will on the horses he buys from Mr. Stanley," Mr. Barnham replied. "I will go now and make the arrangements."

There was a twinkle in his eye as he looked at the Marquis to ask:

"As I am sure, My Lord, you will be in a hurry, you will wish to travel in your Phaeton and drive the new team of chestnuts, and I shall be very surprised if you do not beat your own record to London."

"That is exactly what I intend to do," the Marquis said, "and I hope, Romana, you will not feel nervous if we travel at an almost unprecedented speed."

"I will time you, My Lord," Romana replied, "and the only thing which will make me nervous is if the chestnuts do not come up to scratch!"

"They will do that," the Marquis said, "or I will put them straight into Stanley's sale."

They all laughed and Mr. Barnham thought his two young protégés were behaving exactly in the manner that he wanted them to.

As they journeyed to London Romana knew that she felt very different from the way she had felt on her journey to Sarne.

Then she had been dazed, bewildered, and at the same time frightened until it was hard to think of anything except the pain from the bruise on her cheek.

Now she could laugh and talk with the Marquis without being nervous, and she knew after last night that she was no longer as much afraid of him as she had been before.

It was as if the mere fact that she was cleverer than he in one particular made him less awe-inspiring and less menacing.

She had shown him a poem that her father had translated and he had managed, with some stumbling, to read it in the original Greek, while occasionally admitting frankly, that he had no idea what a certain word meant.

Then as they started on those that were unfinished it seemed to Romana as if they became friendly almost to the point of comradeship.

They argued over the translation.

"You are wrong, I am sure! That is not the right word!" Romana would say.

The Marquis would reply:

"Why not? You will find exactly the same word has been used by your father in another poem."

He was much quicker and more perceptive than she had ever imagined he would be and, when he read aloud some of her father's versions in the poetic form, she thought the depth of his voice and the manner in which he pronounced his words made them sound as if they were set to music.

It was after midnight when the Marquis had glanced inadvertently at the clock and Romana had said hastily:

"Oh, I am sorry! I should have stopped ages ago! I got carried away with Papa's work and I forgot it could not mean the same to you."

"I have enjoyed every moment!" the Marquis said. "And I am telling the truth, not just being polite."

Romana had looked at him searchingly as if she could hardly believe what she heard, then she had smiled.

"I do wish Papa could hear you say that," she said. "He was always so anxious that young men should understand the greatness of Greek thought. He believed it would help them in whatever they did, and especially in politics."

"Are you suggesting that is something in which I should interest myself more than I do already?"

"I think it is important."

"Why?"

"Because at this moment in our history we need strong politicians."

"To combat Napoleon?"

"Of course! We may hate him, we may fear him, but there is no doubt he has a mental and physical strength which is menacing all Europe, and us as well."

The Marquis was surprised. He was not used to women

taking an intelligent interest in politics.

"We have an Armistice," he said at length.

"And how long do you think it is going to last?" Romana enquired.

They began to argue in a spirited fashion, when the clock on the mantlepiece struck one and Romana jumped to her feet.

"Oh, I am sorry!" she cried. "We should have gone to bed a long time ago, but you diverted me onto another subject altogether, and one about which I feel intensely."

"That is obvious," the Marquis said, "and another of your surprises! If there are any more of them you will have me gaping like a yokel or having a heart attack!"

"At least it will be better than watching you stifling your yawns!" she flashed.

"Is that what you saw me doing the first night we were together?"

She gave one of her spontaneous little laughs.

"Oh, no! Then you were blasting me with your eyes and striking at me with your vibrations, and I wanted to run . . away and . . hide somewhere."

There was a little tremor in her voice that told him, although she had spoken jokingly, that she remembered how real it had seemed at the time.

"I hope now you are no longer frightened of me," the Marquis said in a low voice.

She looked up at him and he was almost sure the flicker of fear was no longer there. Then she said:

"You have been so kind . . so understanding about Papa, and I do not think anyone who loves Greek could . . frighten me . . as Lord Kirkhampton did."

"Forget him!" the Marquis said sharply.

"It is what I shall . . try to do," Romana replied.

She gave a little sigh that was one of relief.

"Tonight," she said, "I shall not think about him or about what has . . happened to us. I shall just recite Papa's poems until I fall asleep."

"Then I am sure you will sleep well," the Marquis said. "Good-night, Romana."

He put out his hand and as she laid her fingers on it, he

raised them to his lips.

He felt her quiver, but he thought, although he was not sure, that it was not the same as when she trembled with fear because he was near her.

Then as if she was shy she moved swiftly away from him and left the room before he could speak again.

The Marquis stood at the mantlepiece thinking for a long time before he too, went to bed.

. . . . .

Now intent as he was on driving his horses with remarkable expertise, it was not a moment for conversation.

As he glanced at Romana he saw that she was smiling and he knew she was enjoying herself.

There was nothing the Marquis enjoyed more than trying to beat a record, even if it was his own, and it was with an air of triumph that he drew up outside Sarne House in exactly eleven minutes less time than he had taken on his previous journey.

Romana was looking at his watch which she had held during the whole of the journey.

"You have done it! You have done it!" she cried. "I cannot wait to get back tomorrow and tell Mr. Barnham what we have achieved."

"Barnham is not the only one who will be interested," the Marquis replied. "I heard all the stable-boys at Sarne having bets on how long we would take."

"They should not be encouraged to gamble," Romana said primly, but her eyes were laughing.

Mr. Barnham had arranged for them to have an early dinner and the Marquis would leave immediately afterwards for Baldock.

"You will be able to drive most of the way in day-light, My Lord," he said, "but anyway, if you are delayed, there is a full moon tonight."

The sky was clear and it had been a very warm, sunny day.

After the country London seemed dusty and dirty, and despite the magnificence of Sarne House, Romana was glad that they would be returning to the country.

Mrs. Mayfield was however, delighted to see her.

"You are looking very different from when you left here, M'Lady," she said, "and very much more beautiful, if I may say so,"

"Thank you," Romana answered.

"There's not a sign of the mark on your cheek," Mrs. Mayfield went on. "That's certainly satisfactory, M'Lady."

Romana handed Mrs. Mayfield the shopping list.

"You and I have to go and buy all these things tomorrow, Mrs. Mayfield," she said. "I cannot believe they are necessary, but Mrs. Hughes says I must have them."

"Then there'll be no argument about it," Mrs. Mayfield replied. "And there are several gowns arrived here and only waiting to be conveyed to Your Ladyship at Sarne."

"I cannot believe I really need any more clothes," Romana answered.

"Then you're not like most ladies who never have enough," Mrs. Mayfield replied.

She spoke in a manner which made Romana aware that she was thinking of the other women in whom the Marquis had been interested.

It suddenly struck her that she had not worried so far as to what he thought of her appearance and she wondered for the first time, whether he thought she was pretty.

She was aware that he no longer hated her as he had at first, but he had never paid her a compliment and she thought perhaps she was not the type he admired.

Or else he compared her so unfavourably with the other women in whom he had been interested that he did not even notice her looks or what she was wearing.

She remembered Mr. Barnham saying there had been a great many ladies and many beautiful ones who had wished to marry him.

She supposed they were all of great social importance, perhaps the acclaimed toasts of St. James's. "The Incomparables", as they were called.

"How can I compete with women like that?" she asked herself.

She glanced at herself in the mirror and thought she looked very elegant and very unlike the unfashionably dressed girl who had come from Little Hamble to find work in London, although perhaps in the Marquis's eyes she still looked countryfied.

"We'll buy lots more gowns, Mrs. Mayfield," she said aloud and wondered almost despairingly if they would make any difference.

When she came down to dinner in an extremely pretty gown that had only just arrived at Sarne House, it was to find the Marquis wearing the clothes in which he would drive to Baldock.

"I hope you will forgive me," he said politely, "but as I wish to leave immediately the meal is over I thought I would save time by not having to change again."

"That is sensible," Romana said. "Will it be quite safe for you . . I mean . . when daylight fades?"

"Quite safe," the Marquis replied with a smile. "You heard Mr. Barnham say there is a full moon tonight."

"I know there have been terrible accidents when it is dark," Romana said. "Papa would never drive at night if he could help it."

She was sure as she spoke, that the Marquis would suppose her father would not drive so well or have such good horses as he did.

"You are right about that," she said to his surprise, "but Papa loved good horse-flesh, and when I found after he was dead there was no money left, I blamed myself for not realising how expensive the horses were to keep and how I should have sold quite a number of them when Papa first became ill."

"You were much too young to cope with such things," the Marquis said.

"I think the truth was that my head was in the clouds, and poetry being so beautiful and 'other-worldly' is not very practical."

"One does not expect a woman to be practical," the Marquis answered. "And now, Romana, you can go on being 'other-worldly' while I cope with everything that is material and banal."

"That is exactly what I should like to do," Romana said, "but somehow it sounds rather lazy."

"There are, as it happens, quite a number of practical things for you to do as well," the Marquis said, "like entertaining the Lord Chief Justice, and not forgetting to be nice to the Lord Lieutenant!"

Romana gave a little cry.

"Now you are being horrid! I promise you I will make it up to Lord Lovell the very next time we meet him."

She spoke with so much concern that the Marquis said:

"You need not really worry about him. He is rather an old bore, just as his wife bores me. We do not have to see them more often than is necessary."

"But they are important in the County."

"So am I," the Marquis said, "and so will you be."

"Now you *are* making me nervous," Romana protested. "I am already wondering how I can possibly do all the things Lady Lovell says she wants me to do."

"We will get Barnham to sort out exactly what is necessary and what is not," the Marquis said. "I am not having you bothered with endless committees. They usually involve a great deal of 'talk' and not much 'do'."

Romana laughed.

"I am sure that is true. When Mama helped charities she always found it much easier to go and do things herself rather that sit around a table and decide what should be done."

"We will talk about this on the way home," the Marquis said. "Now I really think I should go."

"Yes, of course," Romana said. "You do not want any port?"

"No. I drink very little when I am driving," the Marquis replied, "and that, I assure you, is the best way to avoid an accident."

He liked the way she smiled at him approvingly.

"I was afraid when I first . . met you," she said, "that you . . drank. Now I realise you are very abstemious."

"You have a great many things to learn about me," the Marquis said, "but I expect that when I am gone you will be thinking only about your father's poetry."

Romana gave a little laugh, but she did not contradict him and he thought that she certainly did not flatter him or overwhelm him with compliments, as his other women had always done.

As he drove away from Sarne House and Romana waved him good-bye from the door-step, he wondered exactly what she did feel about him and knew there were questions to which sooner or later, he would like to have an answer.

When he had gone, feeling rather lonely and flat, Romana went into the Drawing-Room.

For the first time she was able to appreciate the pictures, the beautiful decorations and the flowers that scented the room with their fragrance. She knew they had been hastily arranged once the household knew that they were coming back for the night.

It was all very luxurious and very beautiful. At the same time without the Marquis she felt solitary and unexpectedly lonely.

She had at first hated him so fervently that it had been almost an agony each time she met him, but now she thought he was interesting to talk to and it was exciting in a strange way she could not explain, to have a man all to herself.

'I have a lot to do tomorrow,' she thought. 'I will go to bed and take a book with me, in case I cannot sleep.'

She went into the Library to look for one and thought the whole room seemed redolent of its owner.

There was his monogram surmounted by a crest on the blotter and the ink-pot, on the backs of many of the books and in the plaster-work surmounting the mirror over the fireplace.

It was almost as if he left an atmosphere of himself behind and it was so vivid that she felt almost as if he was beside her.

Hastily because she did not want to think about him so intensely, she chose a book and went upstairs.

A maid was waiting for her, but she then fetched Mrs. Mayfield.

"Your Ladyship's wise to go to bed early now that His Lordship's gone," Mrs. Mayfield said. "We'll be busy tomorrow and anyway, I expect you miss His Lordship. It's hard to be parted when you're only just married."

"Yes . . of course," Romana agreed.

"We were just saying downstairs, M'Lady, that never has there been such an outstandingly handsome couple as yourself and His Lordship. It's happy we are that he's found a wife at last, and he's happier than he's ever been, and that's a fact!"

"Do you really . . think so?" Romana asked slowly.

"There was certainly something wrong when he was here last," Mrs. Mayfield answered. "It must have been the accident you had that upset him, but now he's all smiles and contentment. But there—that's what a happy marriage does for you."

Romana said nothing.

She only wondered when she got to bed whether it would ever be possible for her to make the Marquis happy.

She had certainly never thought it possible three days ago, but last night had been different, very different.

Yet it seemed impossible that she could ever mean anything so important in his life or he in hers.

She read for a little, then she must have fallen asleep.

The next thing she knew was that someone was knocking on her door.

She woke up to find the candle beside her bed was low but was still alight, and for a moment she could not think where she was.

Then she remembered. She was in London.

The knock came again.

"Who is it?" she called.

"It's the nightwatchman, M'Lady."

Romana thought it strange but she was sure he would not be knocking on her door unless it was important.

"Wait a minute!" she called.

She got out of bed and taking up an elegant wrap of satin and lace which Mrs. Mayfield had left over a chair she put it on and slipped her feet into a pair of satin slippers to match.

She went to the door and opened it.

Outside was an old man holding a lantern in his hand.

"Sorry to disturb you, M'Lady."

"What is wrong?" she asked.

"There be a lady 'ere saying she must see you. I told her

Your Ladyship had retired, but she said it were urgent, a matter of life and death!"

"Life and death?" Romana questioned.

"Yes, M'Lady. She said not to wake anybody else, as I wanted to do and no-one must know except me, that she'd called."

"I cannot understand what all this is about," Romana said. "Did you ask the lady's name?"

"Yes, M'Lady, but she wouldn't give it. She says to tell Your Ladyship she came from Dingle Dell."

Romana started.

"Are you sure that is what she said?"

"Yes, M'Lady. Dingle Dell she says."

Romana drew in her breath.

"I will come downstairs," she said to the nightwatchman, "I will come at once."

She knew who had called to see her.

It must be something very important for Nicole to come to Sarne House in the middle of the night!

CHAPTER SIX

"I puts the lady in th' Morning-Room, M'Lady," the nightwatchman said.

Romana did not reply, she was already half-way down the stairs.

She ran down them, seeing that the Hall below was lit only by two candles in one of the silver sconces, and opened the door of the Morning-Room.

Here again the only light was from the candelabrum on the writing-table, but it was enough for her to see a veiled figure standing by the fireplace.

As she came into the room the veil was raised and Romana gave a cry of delight.

"Nicole, dearest! I have wanted so much to see you! Why are you here?"

She did not wait for an answer but ran across the room to put her arms round Nicole and kiss her on the cheek.

Even as she did so, because they were so closely attuned Romana knew that Nicole was perturbed.

"What has happened? Why have you come to see me at this hour of the night?" she asked, before Nicole could speak.

At last it seemed that Nicole found her voice.

"I had to come, and I too have longed to see you, dearest Romana, but eet has been impossible."

"I can understand that," Romana said, "but why now at such a strange time?"

Nicole glanced over her shoulder almost as if she thought somebody was listening.

"I could not come before," she said, "not 'til His Lordship 'ad left, but I knew that I had to warn you."

"Warn me?" Romana repeated, "about what?"

There was an expression on Nicole's face and a note in her voice she did not understand.

Now the French girl said hardly above a whisper:

"We better sit down. I am afraid what I have to say might be overheard."

There was no doubt, Romana thought, that she was very nervous, and Nicole holding her hand, drew her to the sofa so that they sat down side by side.

Nicole was facing the light and Romana could see that she was very pale and there was an expression on her face she did not understand.

However she looked very lovely, her dark hair framed by the veil which streamed over her shoulders making her look almost like a picture of a saint.

"What have you come to tell me?" Romana prompted as Nicole did not speak.

"I had to come," Nicole said again, "and what I have to say may upset you, I not know."

Romana was puzzled, but she said nothing, knowing that Nicole would tell her what had to be told in her own way.

"I have been so ashamed, so humiliated by what happen to you," Nicole said, hardly above a whisper, "but I could not prevent it from happening."

"I understand," Romana said hastily, "of course I understand, but it was frightening, and I thought wicked."

"I thought so too," Nicole agreed. "Now His Lordship has heard that you and ze Marquis are not so unhappy as he hoped."

"How can he have heard that?" Romana enquired.

"He has also learned," Nicole went on as if she had not spoken, "that you are looking very lovely in new gowns."

"I do not understand," Romana said, "who could have talked to him about us?"

Again Nicole looked over her shoulder towards the door.

"He has spies both at Sarne and here."

She spoke in such a low voice that it was almost impossible for Romana to hear her, and yet she did hear.

"Spies?" she exclaimed. "How horrible!"

"That why," Nicole said, "he knows where ze Marquis has gone tonight."

There was something in the way she spoke that warned Romana of what she was about to learn.

"What is , . Lord Kirkhampton going . . to do about it?" she asked, and it was difficult to say the words.

For a moment it seemed as if Nicole found it impossible to reply. Then she said hesitatingly:

"He intend to shoot down ze Marquis when he goes to ze Gallops tomorrow morning!"

Romana gave a little cry.

"It cannot be true! How could any man do anything so diabolical?"

Nicole drew in her breath.

"His Lordship hates ze Marquis—he always has. And I think Romana, his hatred has driven him insane."

"It must have," Romana answered. "How could he plan. . .?"

She stopped and asked in a different tone:

"Tell me what he intends to do."

"He has two men with him," Nicole answered, "who are rough criminals and will do anytheeng for money. They are all riding and they will hide in ze woods near ze Gallops until ze Marquis appears."

"Then they will . . kill him?" Romana said, thinking her voice sounded strange even to herself.

"Or leave him crippled for life."

Nicole gave a cry and put her hands up to her eyes.

"I cannot bear to think of it! Ze Marquis is so magnificent, so admired by everybody except His Lordship."

Romana was hardly listening.

"I must warn him," she said, as if she spoke to herself.

"That ees what I thought you would say," Nicole replied, "but how? As I already tell you, there is a spy somewhere in this house who tells His Lordship everything that happen."

"I will find a way," Romana said.

"I must go back," Nicole cried. "No-one must know I am here. His Lordship would kill me if he thought I betray him!"

"Nicole, what does he mean to you? How could you be with anybody who can do such terrible things?"

Romana spoke passionately and she saw the tears come into Nicole's eyes.

"I am so unhappy," she said.

"I knew it! I knew it the night I arrived. Oh, Nicole, what has happened to you?"

"It ees a long story," Nicole said, "and you have no time now to listen to it. But I am unhappy, dearest Romana, miserably, desperately unhappy, but there ees nothing I can do about it!"

"Why not? What hold has he over you?"

For a moment she thought Nicole was not going to reply, then she said in a broken tone:

"He—married me—at least I thought he did. I was so foolish, so ignorant of ze world, and when he suggested we should have a secret marriage I agree."

There was so much pain in the way she spoke that Romana knew the end of the story before it was told.

"It was only after he had made me his," Nicole said, "that I learn he already had a wife, and that ze Parson who had married us was an actor who needed ze money!"

Romana gave a cry and put her arms round Nicole.

"Dearest, dearest Nicole," she said, "I knew you would not have deliberately done anything wrong or be what the Marquis thought you to be."

"How could I ever tell *mon Père et ma Mère* what happen to me?" Nicole asked brokenly. "Even though His Lordship forbade it at first because he said that for a special reason ze marriage must be kept secret for some months, I nearly disobeyed him and told them I was married to an English nobleman."

"And you loved him?" Romana asked.

"I was fascinated . . mesmerised, if you like, by a man who was so smart, so rich and courted me so romantically."

Nicole gave a little sob.

"Baskets of flowers in ze dressing-room, presents, a carriage to carry me wherever I wanted to go, and he loved me, he really did love me Romana, in his own way, and he still does."

"Is that why you cannot escape?" Romana asked.

"I try, but he said he will kill me if I try again. Oh, Romana, what can I do ? I so ashamed of ze life I am living, so terrified that they might learn in Little Hamble I am not a teacher at a Dancing School, but a prisoner, yes, that is ze word, a prisoner of ze man I hate for what he has done to me."

"Nicole! Nicole!" Romana cried.

Her arms had tightened round Nicole and the tears were running down her cheeks.

For a moment they were both crying against each other. Then Nicole said:

"You must not think about me at ze moment. Save ze Marquis if you can and if you want to. I must go! I pray God that no-one except your nightwatchman knows I have been here."

She sprang to her feet with an urgency as if the dangers of her situation swept over her terrifyingly.

"If I can save the Marquis," Romana said, "I know, Nicole, that he will somehow save you."

"Perhaps no-one can do that," Nicole said miserably, "Seeing what I have become."

Almost incoherent, she moved towards the door and Romana followed her.

When they reached it Nicole lifted her veil again to kiss Romana.

"If you can find happiness with ze Marquis," she said, "that is all that matters. Forget about me."

"I shall never do that," Romana answered, "you are part of my life, my friend, my sister, and we will never lose each other."

Nicole did not reply, she only kissed Romana again, then pulled her veil back over her face.

Outside in the Hall the nightwatchman opened the door for Nicole and Romana could see there was a closed carriage waiting outside.

She did not speak to her again, she merely walked through the open door and without waiting any longer Romana ran up the stairs.

As she went a plan was already forming in her head, but

122

she knew if Nicole was right and there was a spy in the house, she had to be very careful.

It would be no use to warn the Marquis what was waiting for him if Lord Kirkhampton was warned too.

She reached her bedroom and stood for a moment thinking, then went to the wardrobe praying as she did so, that she would find what she wanted.

Her prayer was answered for among the new gowns which Mrs. Mayfield had told her had arrived, was a habit.

She remembered that, when they had ordered the first one which had been finished in a great hurry so that she could take it with her on the day she left for Sarne, Mrs. Mayfield had said something about another to follow and by the mercy of Providence it was here!

Romana wasted no more time, but started to dress.

The habit that she put on was very smart, made in a deep emerald green material, frogged with white braid.

But she was not concerned with her looks, only in getting dressed as quickly as possible and wondering how she could find her way to the stables.

She knew of course, that they would be situated at the back of the house, but she had no idea how to reach them without asking the servants which it would be dangerous to do.

Because of the spy lurking somewhere in the house no-one must know that she had left until enough time elapsed to ensure that she reached the Marquis before anyone could alert Lord Kirkhampton with the knowledge that his victim was aware of his evil plan.

When she was dressed and had found a hat which went with her new habit and even a pair of riding-gloves, she opened the door of her bedroom very quietly and tip-toed along the landing to look down into the Hall, hoping the nightwatchman would not be there.

There was no sign of him and she thought he would be making his rounds.

She slipped down the stairs and went into the Salon where she had sat with the Marquis before dinner.

She remembered it had a long French window which opened into the garden which lay at the back of Sarne

123

House.

She was quite certain that there would be somewhere in the garden a door which opened onto the Mews.

She pulled aside the curtain and saw the moon was already high in the sky and the whole garden was illuminated with a silver light.

She opened the French window and knew now that the only danger was if somebody inside the house saw her and supposed she was a burglar.

However as it was the middle of the night it was very unlikely that anyone would be awake and she hurried across the soft grass keeping to the shadows of the bushes until she reached the end of the garden where there were a number of trees and shrubs.

It took her a little time to find the door that she wanted, but at last it was there and by the light of the moon she could see that it was bolted from the inside.

She pulled back the bolt, the door opened and she stepped out into the Mews.

There were the stables, just as she had anticipated, and now the difficulty was to find someone she could trust.

While she had been dressing she was trying to remember what the Marquis had said about his horses the second night they had dined together at Sarne.

Then suddenly it came back to her.

"I am extremely fortunate in having an excellent trainer at Sarne," he had said. "Cowles is an exceptional man in every way and as good with horse-flesh as I am myself."

Romana had not said she was sure that was impossible as any other woman might have done. She had merely listened and the Marquis had continued:

"In London I have Archer, and I can tell you that if there is a horse on the market that is worth buying, he knows it almost as quickly as the owner decides to sell it."

'Archer! That is his name!' Romana thought.

She crossed the cobbled yard of the Mews and rapped on the door of the closed stable.

For a moment nothing happened, and she was afraid that if she made too much noise somebody at the house would hear her. But there was nothing she could do but knock again.

At last a sleepy voice asked:

"Wot's the matter? Wot's 'appened?"

A moment later the stable-door was opened and a young stable-lad with half-closed eyes and straw in his hair stood looking at her in surprise.

Romana knew that he was on duty in case a carriage or a horse was wanted. He straightened himself and became more alert as she said:

"I want to speak to Mr. Archer immediately. Please fetch him for me!"

"Yus, M'Lidy, right away!" the boy said.

He ran to the back of the stable where there was a very narrow flight of wooden stairs going up into the roof.

Romana stood waiting. There was the movement of horses in the long row of stalls, the smell of hay and leather and she felt too as if she could smell danger—danger to the Marquis.

She had had no time at this moment except to think of the horror that Nicole had related to her, that Lord Kirkhampton meant to strike at his enemy and destroy him.

Now she had a vision of the Marquis lying dead on the ground while his assassins disappeared amongst the trees, never to be caught or punished for their crime.

She was quite certain that was what Lord Kirkhampton planned, and it would be impossible to connect him with what had happened unless either Nicole or his accomplices talked, which she was sure the latter would be too frightened to do.

Even if Nicole gave evidence against him, who would believe her when Lord Kirkhampton denied it?

Because she was only a dancer and 'living in sin', the Court would be prejudiced against her before she even opened her mouth.

Lord Kirkhampton could be certain that he would never be brought to trial, and once the Marquis was dead who would know how to or would trouble themselves to avenge him?

'It must not happen . . it cannot . . happen!' Romana

thought.

At that moment she heard somebody coming down the stairs, then saw a small, wiry little man who in some strange way looked exactly as Romana had expected him to.

He came quickly towards her and lifted his fingers to his forehead.

"Ye wanted me, M'Lady?"

"You are Archer?"

"Yes, M'Lady."

"I want your help," Romana said.

She looked to where the stable-lad was still hovering by the stairs and said:

"I must speak to you alone."

Archer opened the door of the stable and they went outside into the Mews.

"His Lordship is in danger," Romana said. "I have learned that there is a plot to ambush and murder him when he goes to the Gallops tomorrow to watch Mr. Stanley's race-horses. We have to warn him!"

Archer looked considerably startled but at once said firmly:

"I will ride to Baldock and tell His Lordship. I know where he's staying."

"I am coming with you."

Archer did not argue and merely said:

"Very good, M'Lady."

He turned to go back into the stable, but Romana said:

"I think we should go armed. Have you a pistol?"

"Yes, M'Lady. His Lordship always insists that there should be a pistol in every carriage, an' I've a small one that'll suit Your Ladyship."

"Thank you," Romana said, "and now let us hurry! There is no time to be lost."

She had noticed while she was dressing that the clock on the mantelpiece in her bedroom showed the time as being a few minutes after two o'clock.

She was not certain at what time the Marquis would go to the Gallops but she knew it would be as early as possible so as to give himself plenty of time to inspect the horses before they returned to their stables for the sale.

126

Quite suddenly she felt frantically that she might already be too late to save him and when she arrived at Baldock she would find him dead with no sign of the men who had killed him.

With difficulty she prevented herself from crying out at Archer to hurry. She knew he was saddling the horses as quickly as he could and she had no desire to inform the stable-lad who was helping him, of her sense of urgency.

Nicole had said there was a spy at Sarne House and another at Sarne in the country. How could that have happened? How could anyone be so disloyal as to betray their master?

Yet there was always someone who was greedy for money, always someone weak enough to be bribed, and those were the people whom Lord Kirkhampton had paid to turn traitor.

The first horse was ready and the stable-lad led it out into the yard and up to the mounting-block while Archer saddled a horse for himself.

The one he had chosen for Romana was a magnificent stallion and obviously very fresh, for he bucked to show his independence and Romana had a little difficulty in getting into the saddle.

But once she was there, she knew she could handle the horse and he too was aware of it.

Archer came out to join her and without saying a word she started off down the Mews and he caught up with her at the end of it.

He held out his hand towards her and she saw that in it was a small pistol, a neat weapon that could easily be used by a woman.

"I've loaded it, M'Lady."

"Thank you," Romana replied and slipped it into the pocket of her habit.

Then they moved swiftly through the deserted streets, Archer leading the way until they were out of the city and heading North. Then they rode side by side.

"Will it take us long?" Romana asked raising her voice so that he could hear what she said above the noise of the horses' hoofs.

"Under three hours, M'Lady, across country."

Romana did not comment on the fact that she knew Lord Kirkhampton would also be travelling across country with his cut-throats beside him, but she wondered what would happen if they should meet.

Archer led her over the open land and fields, and they saw no-one for the first two hours, then the night began to fade and the first light of dawn appeared in the East.

It was now that Romana began to push her horse harder than she had done previously.

She was certain the Marquis would be up very early and she had to reach him before he left the Inn.

She felt the fear of being too late was constricting her breath, and there was a heaviness in her breasts which she knew was caused by fear.

"Oh, God .. let me be in time .. please let me be in time," she prayed.

As she sent the prayer from her it struck her that only a few days ago she had been praying that the Marquis would die.

"I would not want any man to die in such a manner," she told herself, "and .. especially not the .. Marquis."

She thought because he was so magnificent, so strong, and so athletic that it would be a tragedy to see him cut down and know that he had met his death long before his time.

Then she asked herself what would it mean to her personally, and was afraid of the answer.

. . . . . .

The Marquis woke early not only, he thought, because he was anxious to be at the Gallops but also because the bed in *The Green Dragon* was certainly not as comfortable as the beds in any of his own houses.

He disliked Inns and never stayed in one, if it could possibly be avoided.

But he had deliberately not accepted the invitation to stay with Mr. Stanley, which he found was also included in the letter which had given him the details of the sale. For several reasons he thought it might prove embarrassing.

He knew of old that, when his friends had something to

sell, because he was so wealthy they always pressurised him to buy more than he actually wanted.

He also wished to inspect the horses with a clear mind and knew it was difficult to do so, if he had already been told so much, true or false, about their progress that it might be inclined to blind his judgement.

Mr. Barnham, who knew his feelings on these occasions, had been quite right in expecting he would stay at *'The Green Dragon'* and although the accommodation was not particularly comfortable, it was passable and, after all, as the Marquis told himself, it was only for one night.

He had just got out of bed when his valet came into the room carrying a jug of hot shaving-water and bringing him the clothes he would wear.

"What is the time, Jarvis?" the Marquis enquired.

"Five o'clock exactly, M'Lord, the time Your Lordship asked me to waken you."

"Good!" the Marquis exclaimed. "You have told them to provide me with breakfast?"

"It'll be ready in ten minutes, M'Lord."

The Marquis thought he could always rely on his valet, who had been with him for a number of years and next to himself was the most punctual man in the whole country.

The Marquis was used to dressing quickly and despised the Dandies who spent the entire morning fussing over the style of their cravats and complaining about the polish on their boots.

In exactly ten minutes he walked down the oak staircase to the private parlour where his breakfast was waiting, looking as immaculate as any Beau who had taken hours to array himself.

When he had eaten well but swiftly, the Marquis thanked the land-lord, who was bowing obsequiously at the door, for his accommodation, and swung himself into the saddle of the horse that was waiting for him.

He had arranged yesterday evening when he returned to Sarne House that while he would drive in his Phaeton to Baldock, a groom would go ahead with a horse for him to ride in the morning.

Archer, not accompanying his master, as he usually did, had sent a groom in his place.

"This be a opportunity for Ben, M'Lord," Archer had explained. "He's keen, and it'll be good for 'im to handle two spirited horses on his own."

"Let us hope he gets them safely to Baldock," the Marquis said dryly.

"He'll do that all right, M'Lord, and 'though I'd like to come with Your Lordship, I think Red Rufus has a touch of pneumonia, and there's no-one I can really trust wi' him."

"I understand, Archer," the Marquis said. "At the same time I would have appreciated your opinion with regard to Mr. Stanley's horses."

"I've seen most of 'em already," Archer replied, "and I've made a list of the ones I think Your Lordship might like to buy."

"You are always efficient, Archer, and you know I value your judgement."

"Your Lordship might like others more than the one's I've suggested, M'Lord," Archer said, "but I think I've listed most of those worth having."

"I am sure you have," the Marquis replied.

He put the list in his pocket and was sure that Archer's advice would be good.

Now he looked at Ben who was a fresh-faced country lad of about twenty-one, and he thought from the way he was riding that Archer's confidence in him was justified.

The Marquis not only liked to have superlative horses, he also liked outstanding grooms in attendance upon him, and he thought that Ben would be an asset.

He was intending to enlarge his stable quite considerably, not only with Stanley's horses, but with a number of others he hoped would be in the market before the end of the summer.

He rode down a street in Baldock, then took to the fields which he knew stretched for about a mile, leading to a wood beyond which were the Gallops.

As it was so early there was a mist rising from the fields and he knew the trunks of the trees would be enveloped in white.

The air was fresh and the sun as it rose seemed to have a radiance about it which made the Marquis feel unexpectedly happy.

In fact he felt at peace with the world, and a lark rising ahead of him, sent a paean of joy to the sky which he felt was echoed in his own mind.

He found himself thinking of one of the passages from Sophocles he had read with Romana.

> "..................... *patrolling Night*
> *Breaks off her rounds to let the Dawn ride in*
> *On silver horses lighting up the sky."*

"What an extraordinary thing," he said to himself, "that after the unpleasant things I thought about Romana, I find that she is imbued with the beauty of Greece."

He was aware that although he had half-forgotten it that such beauty of thought and mind had been very much a part of his life when he was at Oxford.

It was his Greek studies that had aroused in him a desire, if not to go out and conquer the world, at least to achieve something in it.

In fact, he thought with a slight smile, all that he had achieved so far in the world of sport might almost be attributed to the ambitions aroused in him by the poems of Pindar.

He knew they had fired his imagination. After he had left Oxford he had forgotten the inspiration, but his desire to excel in so many ways had remained.

"Who could have guessed," he asked, "that the woman I should marry in such strange circumstances should prove to be Arnold Wardell's daughter?"

He found some more lines turning over in his mind and thought that strangely enough, although there appeared to be no connection, they reminded him of Romana.

> "For in your gift are all our mortal joys,
> And every sweet thing, be it wisdom, beauty,
> Or glory, that makes rich the soul of man,"

He wondered if Romana would ever make 'rich the soul of man', then told himself quickly that he should be thinking of the horses he was going to buy!

He and Ben had covered half the distance to the wood when Ben looked back over his shoulder.

"There's someone a-coming after us, M'Lord," he said.

The Marquis was not interested.

He did not think it was very likely that it would be anyone who wanted him. Yet he might not be the only person interested in Stanley's horses, who desired to see them before the sale.

The idea annoyed him and he spurred his horse to go quicker. Then Ben exclaimed:

"Looks like Mr. Archer behind us, M'Lord."

"Nonsense!" the Marquis started to say, but he looked back and recognised not only Archer but Romana.

He drew in his horse and waited, wondering what in the world could have induced Romana to join him from London, knowing that she and Archer must have travelled half the night to be here so early.

Romana cantered up to him and as she drew in her horse he saw that she was very pale and her eyes seemed to fill her whole face.

"Thank God we are in time!" she exclaimed. "When we reached the Inn and found that you had already gone, I was terrified we were too late!"

"In time for what?" the Marquis asked.

"It is . . Lord Kirkhampton," she explained. "He is waiting for you in the wood with two men. He intends to . . kill you!"

The Marquis stared at her as if he thought she had taken leave of her senses.

"What are you saying?" he asked. "I cannot believe this is not some kind of joke."

"No . . it is true," Romana said urgently. "Lord Kirkhampton has hired two felons who will do . . anything for . . money and he intends that they should . . kill you!"

There was no mistaking the sincerity in her voice and that she was really frightened.

For a moment the Marquis looked at her without

132

speaking. Then he said:

"If that is so, then we must certainly give him a surprise!"

He moved his horse to go close to Archer who was speaking to Ben.

"You understand why you are here, Archer?"

"Yes, M'Lord. Her Ladyship told me."

"Have you a weapon with you?"

"Yes, M'Lord, and I brought one for Ben and, in case you were not armed, one for Your Lordship."

The Marquis smiled.

"I thought I was going to the Gallops, Archer, not to a shooting-match."

"That's what it looks like being, M'Lord."

"So I understand."

The Marquis took the pistol that Archer handed him.

It was quite a small one, a little larger than the one Archer had given to Romana, but still a deadly weapon, especially in the hands of a man who was a crack shot.

"Where do you think they will be?" the Marquis asked.

"I was thinking o' that as I was a-coming here," Archer said. "I know exactly, M'Lord, where I would be waiting myself if I was setting up an ambush."

"Then explain to me what we have to expect," the Marquis said.

The three men talked together while Romana on her horse stood a little apart.

She had been so afraid that she would be too late to save the Marquis, and now she had found him in time, she felt suddenly limp as if the urgency which had sustained her during the long ride from London, had been a prop that was no longer required.

She remembered the relief she had felt as she and Archer entered the field which led towards the wood and she had seen the Marquis in the distance and known that he was still alive.

The vision that had haunted her all the way from London of him lying bleeding on the ground in the wood vanished and instead she saw his broad shoulders silhouetted against the morning mist and the manner in which he rode a horse that made him seem as if he was an actual part of the

133

animal.

'I have saved him!' she thought thankfully.

Then she remembered that Lord Kirkhampton was still waiting.

Because she was afraid she moved her horse beside the Marquis to say:

"Surely now we have warned you, it would be best to go home!"

"And have him waiting for me on another occasion?" the Marquis asked. "No, Romana, this is something I have to face and now is the right moment."

She remembered how he had wanted to fight Lord Kirkhampton when he realised what had happened to him when he was drugged, and how Mr. Barnham had persuaded him not to do so.

Now his hand was forced.

To run away would achieve nothing and would certainly be very cowardly.

The Marquis was aware that Romana was looking at him with an almost desperate expression on her face.

He smiled at her.

"Trust me," he said.

"They may . . kill you . . or wound you," Romana said, almost beneath her breath.

"I shall try to prevent them from doing either," the Marquis replied. "But now I want you to come to the edge of the wood and remain in the shelter of the trees on this side. On no account are you to follow us or come into danger. Do you understand?"

Romana nodded. She could not trust her voice.

"I will not let you down," the Marquis said, "and remember Pindar said:

> *"But violence brings to ruin even*
> *The boastful hard heart, soon or late."*

"I will . . try to remember that," Romana said, "and I shall pray . . I shall pray that . . you will be . . safe."

Her eyes met the Marquis's as she spoke, and it seemed as if suddenly both of them were very still.

Then he turned away to speak with Archer and the three men moved without haste towards the wood, Romana following them.

The Marquis was obviously planning exactly what he would do, and while he entered the wood at the centre Archer went to the right and Ben to the left.

As he reached the first clump of trees the Marquis turned in his saddle to point with his hand, and Romana knew he indicated where she was to stop and wait while he went ahead.

The Marquis moved very slowly through the thickness of the wood, not keeping to the path which ran through the centre of it, but zig-zagging amongst the tree-trunks.

Suddenly just ahead of him he heard the faint whinny of a horse and knew where his assailants were waiting.

Romana had stopped where the Marquis had indicated. But she very soon knew that nothing could make her stay there, and wait, wondering what was happening and not knowing until it was all over, whether Lord Kirkhampton had won or lost.

She saw a fallen trunk of a tree on the ground and slipping from the saddle, tied her horse's reins to it, then entered the wood on foot.

The ground beneath the trees was sandy and she walked almost silently, keeping as the Marquis had done, away from the path and moving from tree to tree.

Then a little way in front of her she could see the Marquis on his horse, and with a stab of fear, realised that just ahead of him there was a man with a handkerchief tied over the lower part of his face, in the manner of a Highwayman.

She knew this must be one of Lord Kirkhampton's accomplices.

Then by moving a little to the right she saw on the other side of the path a man who was undoubtedly Lord Kirkhampton.

Like herself he was not on horse-back, but was hiding behind a tree. But there was no mistaking from his height, his broad shoulders and the dark hair that she could see beneath his high hat that he was the man who had forced her into marriage with the Marquis.

As she realised who he was, she heard the Marquis say with a note of amusement in his voice:

"Stand and deliver!"

The man to whom he was speaking was on horse-back. He started violently and fired, but his bullet went wide and as the Marquis fired in reply, he toppled from the saddle.

There was another shot a little further down the wood followed by a second and Romana thought that Archer or Ben was engaging the third man.

Then with a sense of horror she saw Lord Kirkhampton raise his pistol and knew he was aiming at the Marquis.

He himself was completely protected by the tree-trunk behind which he was hiding while the Marquis on his horse silhouetted against the branches, was an easy target.

It was then that Romana hardly thinking what she was doing, and acting instinctively, drew the pistol from her pocket.

She had a feeling that she only had a split second before Lord Kirkhampton would fire, and without deliberately aiming, just bringing down the pistol as her father had taught her to do, she pressed the trigger.

For one frantic moment she thought she had missed. Then Lord Kirkhampton's arm dropped. He must have pulled the trigger for there was an explosion and a bullet hit the ground as he collapsed slowly, very slowly, his body sliding down the trunk of the tree.

For a moment Romana could not believe that it had happened, but felt that she had dreamed it.

Then as she moved onto the path, the Marquis rode towards her.

"What are you doing here? Who were you shooting at?" he asked sharply.

Then he saw Lord Kirkhampton's hand on the ground, his pistol still in it and he dismounted from his horse.

Holding onto the bridle he walked forward to look at Lord Kirkhampton, knowing without inspecting him further that he was dead.

Romana's bullet had shot him through the throat and the blood was staining his white cravat in a crimson flood.

The Marquis's eyes met Romana's.

"He was just . . about to . . fire at you," she said, as if she must excuse herself.

"I did not expect him to hide behind a tree!" the Marquis remarked, "but it was typical of the swine's behaviour."

He spoke contemptuously and Romana knew that, worse than murder, Lord Kirkhampton's behaviour had been unsportsmanlike.

Then as she still looked at the Marquis, feeling as if everything that had happened was unreal, he said quietly:

"Thank you, Romana. I realise you have saved my life."

As if she could hardly believe that he was safe, she glanced round in case there should be anyone else aiming at him through the trees.

"All three are accounted for," the Marquis said reassuringly, "and now I think I should take you away from this unsavoury spot."

He took the pistol from her hand as he spoke and put it into his pocket.

Then he put his arm round her shoulders as if he felt she needed support and started to walk along the path, leading his horse at the same time.

Now it was over Romana had an almost irrepressible impulse to burst into tears.

She could not realise that she had killed a man, that was immaterial. What had shaken her was that for one terrifying moment she had thought Lord Kirkhampton would kill the Marquis and she would not be able to save him.

It suddenly struck her that she had saved Nicole too and she was free.

"You have a lot to tell me," the Marquis said, "and I have a great deal to say to you, Romana. But I think first, as you must have been riding for a long time, you need something to eat. Are you able to ride?"

"Yes . . I will be . . all right," Romana said. "It was . . all such a . . shock."

"I can understand that," the Marquis said quietly, "but I have never known any woman to show such courage, unless of course, she came from Ancient Greece."

With an effort Romana forced a smile to her lips.

She knew the Marquis was trying to take away the tension of the moment and prevent her from feeling horrified at what she had done.

They emerged from the wood into the field. The Marquis looked at Romana for a long moment, then he picked her up in his arms and sat her on the saddle of his own horse.

She gave a little murmur of protest, but before she could say anything they were joined by Archer and Ben, the latter with an expression of wild excitement on his face.

He had killed his first man and he was proud of it.

"Bring Her Ladyship's horse with you," the Marquis said, and swung himself on the saddle behind Romana.

He put his arm round her holding her tightly against him and it gave her a comforting feeling of protection and security.

"You are . . safe," she murmured almost beneath her breath as they moved over the field back the way they had come.

"I am safe, thanks to you," he said quietly.

They rode on for a few seconds without speaking. Then Romana suddenly said:

"The Gallops! You were going to the Gallops. Had you forgotten?"

"As a matter of fact I had," the Marquis replied.

He pulled in his horse and Archer and Ben came up to him.

"Give Ben Her Ladyship's horse, Archer," he said. "Go to the Gallops. If there are any other horses you fancy, add them to those you have already marked on your list. Make my apologies to Mr. Stanley, and buy anything you think I would buy if I was present."

"You'll not be coming to the sale, M'Lord?"

"No," the Marquis replied, "I am taking Her Ladyship back to London. I think she has had enough excitement for one day."

Archer handed Ben the reins of Romana's horse.

"I'll do my best, M'Lord," he said, and touching his cap with his whip he rode back towards the wood.

"You must not . . miss the sale," Romana protested. "I shall be . . all right."

"Strange though it seems," the Marquis replied, "I find you more important at the moment than any number of race-horses."

He spoke lightly, but his arm tightened around her and Romana felt as if something very strange had happened to her heart.

CHAPTER SEVEN

Romana awoke and felt as if she had been asleep for a very long time.

She remembered how exhausted she had felt when after driving at a great speed, the Marquis had reached London in what she was sure was another record.

She had realised his anxiety to get back as quickly as possible to Sarne House was not entirely on her account, but also because he was aware it would be unwise to stay in the vicinity of Baldock whereby he might in some way, be connected, when Lord Kirkhampton was found, with his death.

There was every chance, Romana thought, that the bodies of the three men in the wood would not be discovered for some time, perhaps even for days.

But the horses would wander away and sooner or later it would be brought to the notice of the Police that there were three dead bodies to be identified and it would then be found that one of them was a nobleman.

There were various explanations, Romana reasoned, that would be brought to the attention of the Magistrates.

First, that as Lord Kirkhampton was in the company of men who were obviously of criminal type, they had shot him, although it would seem strange that he had managed to account for both of them.

Secondly, the deaths of all three men might be attributed to Highwaymen. The road North from London was notorious for its footpads and Highwaymen, who not only robbed coaches but were known as bullion thieves.

Any of these might have come into conflict with Lord Kirkhampton and there was no reason whatsoever that his death should be attributed to the Marquis.

At the same time, it was prudent to get as far from the wood as possible, and Romana could understand why when they reached 'The Green Dragon' the Marquis had sent for coffee and something for her to eat while he ordered his Phaeton to be brought round immediately.

The horses, having rested since his arrival the night before, were fresh and responded to the speed that he required of them.

Yet because he was always so solicitous for his horses Romana had heard him give Ben strict instructions before he left, that the horse she had ridden down from London was to be brought back slowly and quietly.

She drank the coffee gratefully knowing she was thirsty.

She had however, only been able to nibble at the breakfast-dishes which the landlord put in front of her, in the private room.

All she could keep thinking of, was that the Marquis was safe and she had managed to save him.

But she knew she would never forget that terrifying moment when she had found on arrival at 'The Green Dragon' that he had already left, and she thought her journey had been in vain.

Now, remembering the fear that swept over her so that it had been difficult not to scream out loud, she was aware the memory of it had been superseded by a very different emotion when she rode back in the Marquis's arms from the wood to the Inn.

It seemed extraordinary when she had hated the Marquis so violently, shrinking from him in horror in case he might touch her even inadvertently, that it had been a happiness difficult to express in words to know that she was in his arms and she no longer had to be afraid of him.

"How could I have changed my opinion of him so completely?" Romana asked herself.

She knew that in a way she could not attempt to put into words he had, since they had translated the Greek together, become identified with everything the poems aroused in her mind and in her heart.

Her studies of Greek with her father had given her an

idealism besides an inspiration that was so much a part of her whole being that it was impossible to analyse what they made her feel within herself.

In fact they were herself, and just as her father had when he was alive, filled her whole life, so in some extraordinary manner she could not even for the moment contemplate the Marquis seemed to have taken his place.

Now the light that was Greek and which had inspired her with its beauty and its divine power linked her spiritually with the Marquis so that she felt as if she was a part of him and he of her.

It was because she knew that he would understand and believe her that she said as they neared London:

"I must go at once to see Nicole."

She thought he might be surprised, but instead he replied:

"I have the idea that it was Nicole de Prêt who warned you that Kirkhampton intended to kill me."

"Yes, it was," Romana replied. "She came to Sarne House last night at two o'clock. She was veiled and she sent the nightwatchman to wake me."

"Were you frightened?"

"Not when he told me a lady wished to see me who, although she would not give her name, said I would know who she was when he said the words 'Dingle Dell'."

The Marquis raised his eyebrows and Romana explained:

"It was a special place in the wood where we always played together."

"So you knew it was Nicole de Prêt downstairs."

"I ran down," Romana replied, "and found her in the Morning-Room."

"You must have been astonished to see her."

"I could not understand why she had come at such an odd hour until she explained that Lord Kirkhampton had just left her to ride to Baldock and wait in the wood to kill you on the way to the Gallops."

"How did he know where I was going?"

"That is just what I was going to tell you. Nicole told me that he has a spy at Sarne House and another in the country."

"A spy?" the Marquis exclaimed.

"I was horrified too, that any of your servants could betray you in such a way."

"I can hardly believe it!" the Marquis said. "Kirkhampton must have paid them a lot of money. I would have trusted any of those I employ with my life."

"That is . . exactly what you were . . doing," Romana said.

The Marquis's lips tightened and because she knew it hurt him to think of such treachery she said quickly:

"It must be one of the younger servants. I am sure those who have served you for many years and consider your house their home too, would never stoop to anything so disloyal."

"It was brave of Nicole to come to you," the Marquis remarked.

"Very brave," Romana agreed, "because she told me that if Lord Kirkhampton . . found out he would . . kill her!"

"At least we have saved her from that."

"We have saved her in another way as well," Romana replied. "She told me that Lord Kirkhampton 'married' her, or she thought he had."

"Married her?"

There was no doubt of the surprise in the Marquis's voice and he turned his head for a moment to look at Romana.

"I told you she is pure and good," she said. "She would never have done . . anything so wicked as . . what you . . suggested."

"So Kirkhampton pretended to marry her!"

"He said there was a reason for them to have a secret marriage and it was only later that she discovered the Parson who had married them was in fact, an actor."

"That is just the sort of behaviour one might expect from an outsider like Kirkhampton!"

"Nicole was so . . upset when she discovered the truth that she tried to leave him, but he would not let her go. He threatened her and she was afraid . . terribly afraid of him . . as I was."

"She is free of him now," the Marquis remarked.

"That is what I was thinking, and . . perhaps you will . . allow me to . . help her."

"Of course."

Romana's eyes lit up.

"That is kind and . . generous of you."

"Shall I say that I am apologising for my suspicions?"

"I can understand now that they . . appeared to be . . justified," Romana said in a low voice.

They drove for a little while in silence. Then the Marquis said:

"As I think you are very tired, I want you to rest and allow me to find Nicole de Prêt and tell her what has happened. May I do that?"

"Yes, of course," Romana replied. "I admit to being somewhat exhausted."

It was not only the long ride and the journey back to London which had depleted her strength. It was, she knew, the fact that she was still feeling the shock of having killed a man and seeing him lying dead.

However justified her action might have been, it was still terrifying to know that one moment Lord Kirkhampton had been living and breathing and attempting to murder the Marquis, and the next he had been just an inanimate body on the ground, with blood seeping over his white cravat.

As if the Marquis understood what she was feeling, he said in a voice that was more kindly than he had ever used to her before:

"Do not think about what has happened. Go to bed and recite your father's poems to yourself. Think of the light shining on Greece when, as they believed, Apollo poured across the sky healing everything he touched and defying the powers of darkness."

Romana gave a little murmur which was one of delight and the Marquis said:

"Whatever happens to us in our lives we know in our minds that we can still find and see beauty, and that is what really matters."

Romana looked at him in astonishment, then she asked:

"How can you say . . such things? How can you . . think in the same way that my father . . did and I only just be . . aware of it?"

The Marquis smiled.

"I think I am only just aware of it myself. In the circle of friends in which I have moved these last few years they would think I was mad if I spoke to them as I am speaking to you now."

"To me it is a . . revelation," Romana murmured.

She felt as if her heart was singing because the Marquis understood and she was no longer alone as she had thought herself to be ever since her father had died.

Now she thought of what he had said, and the look in his eyes when on reaching Sarne House, he had sent her upstairs to bed.

She had felt a strange excitement creep over her and knew it was happiness—a happiness she had never expected to feel the first night when she had slept in the Sarne bed she was in now.

Then insidiously, almost as if the thought had come into her mind like the serpent entering the Garden of Eden, it struck her that the Marquis had been very eager to go and see Nicole!

She had forgotten for the moment, that the reason the Marquis was in Nicole's house in the first place, was because he had been attracted to her.

He had asked her out to supper and it was she who had suggested on Lord Kirkhampton's instigation, that he should dine at home with her.

Because the Marquis had been so unkind about Nicole when he had been trapped into marriage, Romana had forgotten that it was because he had found her so attractive as a dancer at Covent Garden that he had pursued her.

Perhaps, she now told herself, the reason why he was so willing to go and tell Nicole Lord Kirkhampton was dead was that he could now renew his 'courtship', if that was the right word.

Romana shut her eyes and turned her face against the pillow.

Instead of the happiness and the light of Greece that the

Marquis had given her, there was only once again the darkness of being alone and, worst of all, of losing him.

She had always thought that Nicole was so much more attractive than herself. She danced better, was more amusing and certainly more sophisticated in being able to entertain a man like the Marquis.

'He will love her.' Romana suddenly thought, 'and he will no longer want to talk to me, translate the Greek, or even ride with me.'

She gave a little cry of sheer misery and as she did so she knew that she loved him.

She supposed she had been very stupid not to realise it before, not to know why she felt so frightened that he might be killed by Lord Kirkhampton and that the reason she wanted to save him was that he meant so much to her.

The manner in which she had saved him from being murdered and the emotions that she could not explain to herself when he had carried her away from the wood on the front of his saddle were at this moment all too easy to understand.

It was love! Love for a man who had hated her as she had hated him. Now he was free from being obliged to stay at her side as had been necessary while Lord Kirkhampton was alive.

"Nicole is free! The Marquis is free!" Romana murmured, "and I am a . . prisoner of my own . . heart."

That she knew was indisputably true, even though it seemed impossible!

How could she have changed so completely from the woman who hated the man to whom she had been married by force, to one who loved him with every nerve of her body, with every breath she drew?

Love!

It seemed to encompass her to the point where it superseded everything else.

She wanted to cry out in agony because it hurt her as nothing had ever hurt her before.

"Why did I not . . know? Why did I not . . understand?" she asked.

She thought of the hours she had spent alone at Sarne

146

with the Marquis and had been too stupid not to prize and treasure them.

She had driven back to London beside him and it had been a happiness like brilliant sunshine to be in his company, but she had not realised it was love that made her feel and think they were very close.

Now she had lost him!

How would he be able to resist Nicole with her slanting dark eyes, her white skin and her exquisite grace?

"They will be happy . . very happy . . together," Romana told herself, "and they will forget me as I am no . . longer of any . . importance."

She felt the tears gather in her eyes and she tried to tell herself that because she loved Nicole she should be glad that she could be happy after being so miserable with a man like Lord Kirkhampton.

And because she loved the Marquis she should want him too, to find happiness!

"I would have . . tried to make him . . happy," she murmured, "but compared to Nicole . . what have I to . . offer him?"

The answer to that question merely made her more miserable than she was already.

Nicole and the Marquis!

She could see them almost as if they stood side by side, in front of her, and no couple could be more attractive, more beautiful—he in his strong athletic way like Apollo and she exquisite, like Aphrodite.

Nicole would not be able to talk to him about Greece since the subject had never interested her, but Romana told herself they would have so many other things in common of which she was ignorant.

The door opened softly and Romana asked:

"Who is it?"

"I was just wondering, M'Lady, if you were awake," Mrs. Mayfield replied. "I've brought Your Ladyship's tea."

"Thank you," Romana said.

Mrs. Mayfield came into the room and drew back the curtains.

It was late in the afternoon and there were shadows beneath the trees in the centre of the Square, but the sunshine was still bright.

Yet Romana knew why it did not seem as brilliant and as glittering to her as it had been when she had driven back from Baldock with the Marquis.

She sat up in bed and Mrs. Mayfield put a tray beside her on which was a silver tea-pot, cream-jug and sugar-basin engraved with the Marquis's crest, a cup and saucer and other china of Crown Derby.

"I've brought you some sandwiches to eat, M'Lady, and there's scones and cakes of every description, should you fancy them."

"I am not hungry, thank you," Romana replied. "Only a little thirsty."

She poured herself a cup of tea while Mrs. Mayfield tidied the room. Then she asked:

"Is His Lordship . . back yet?"

"Not yet, M'Lady."

Romana put down her cup and lay back against the lace-edged pillows.

He had been with Nicole for a long time, she thought. Perhaps they were planning their future together, a future in which there would be no part for her to play.

"Now you try and get some more sleep, M'Lady," Mrs. Mayfield said. "You look tired out, and that's a fact! You've plenty of time for a nap before dinner."

Romana did not reply and as Mrs. Mayfield carried the tray away and shut the door behind her, she thought it would not matter what she looked like.

She was quite certain that even if the Marquis did return in time for dinner, he would be thinking only of Nicole.

She tried to repeat some of her father's poems, but none of them seemed to express her feelings nor for the moment could they bring her the comfort that they had always done in the past.

"All I want is that the Marquis should come back, and as that is impossible, I am left with an . . empty world in which I am so very . . very . . alone."

Then as once again she felt the tears prick her eyes there

was a knock on the door and before she could reply the Marquis came in.

She felt for a moment as if because she had wanted him so agonisingly he was only a figment of her imagination.

Then as he smiled at her and walked towards the bed, she knew he was real.

"Mrs. Mayfield tells me you have been asleep," he said. "Are you rested?"

"Yes . . thank you." ·

Because she was so glad to see him, because for the moment nothing mattered except that he was there, she put out her hand and he took it in both of his.

As she touched him she felt herself quiver and he must have been aware of it, for his hold tightened and she thought he looked deep into her eyes as if he was searching for something.

Then he said:

"It has seemed a long time since I washed and dressed this morning to go to the Gallops, a great many things have happened since then. Will you allow me to take off my driving-clothes before I tell you what I know you are curious to hear?"

'Y . yes . . of course."

Romana found it hard to find words and was conscious only of his eyes looking into hers and the closeness of his hands.

"I will not be long," he smiled.

He walked across the room to leave not by the door through which he had entered, but by another which Romana knew communicated with his bedroom.

She watched the door close behind him, then she found herself wondering desperately what he was going to tell her.

He had been such a long time with Nicole. They must have found a great deal to talk about!

She wondered how much he would tell her of what had actually been said, but at least he was back with her, and that was an inexpressible joy in itself.

She could only watch the door, longing with an intensity which nothing could suppress to see him again.

She had begun to think that he had in fact, forgotten her

when at last he returned.

Now the sunshine was no longer pouring through the windows but instead the room seemed a little dim and very quiet, almost as if it waited like a prelude to a play, for the drama go begin.

The Marquis was here.

He walked towards her and she saw that he was wearing not the clothes she had always seen him in before, but a long silk robe which made him look even taller than he usually did.

But it was impossible for Romana to look at anything except his face while her eyes searched his, wondering what he had to tell her.

He reached the bed to stand looking down at her hair falling over her shoulders, golden against the pillows, and the fine lace-trimmed nightgown which barely concealed the curves of her breasts.

For a moment he seemed to hesitate, then he said:

"I am rather tired, Romana, and as I want to rest, do you think I might do so with you?"

For a moment she started, then she said quickly:

"Y . yes . . of . . course."

She moved a little towards the centre of the bed as she did so thinking that the Marquis would lie on top of the lace cover, but to her surprise he took off his silk robe and raising the sheet, got in beside her.

Romana drew in her breath. Her heart began to thump violently in her breast and she was trembling, but not with fear.

"That is more comfortable," the Marquis said with satisfaction as he lent back against the pillows. "Now we can talk and I can tell you everything which I am sure you are curious to know."

As he spoke in an almost impersonal manner Romana thought she should be as casual as he appeared to be and she said, although there was a distinct tremor in her voice:

"Of . . course I am . . curious . . was Nicole . . very pleased?

As she spoke, she thought it would be impossible for Nicole to be anything else. She was free of Lord

Kirkhampton and now the Marquis could be hers.

"I think 'pleased' is rather an inadequate word with which to describe what Nicole feels," the Marquis replied.

"She was . . surprised to see . . you?"

Romana could not help asking the question.

She was wondering if Nicole had been as delighted to see the Marquis as he had been to see her.

"I think," the Marquis said, "she had been waiting and praying about what would be the outcome of my encounter with Kirkhampton."

"You . . told her that she was . . free of him?"

"I think that is what she anticipated would happen once I learnt of the ambush. It was very brave of her to come and warn you."

Romana clasped her fingers together.

The Marquis had thought that Nicole was brave and doubtless he had kissed her when he told her so.

There was a silence which the Marquis broke by turning to look at Romana beside him.

"What is worrying you?" he asked.

"How . . how do know a . anything is . . worrying me?" Romana parried.

"Perhaps like the Greeks I am being perceptive," he said. "There is something wrong, and I want to know what it is."

"It is . . nothing. . ." Romana began.

Then her eyes met his and she found she could not lie.

The Marquis had turned round so that his face was near to hers.

"There is something wrong," he said. "When I left you were happy. I could feel it vibrating from you. But now you are vibrating something very different. Tell me what it is, Romana. I want to know."

With an effort Romana took her eyes from his and looked across the room towards the window.

"I was . . thinking," she said in a very small voice, "that now you are . . free of Lord Kirkhampton . . there will be nothing to . . stop me from . . going home . . as I wished to do . . before."

"Is that what you really want to do?" the Marquis

enquired.

She knew if she told the truth she would say that it was the last thing she wanted. She wanted to stay with him, and to leave would be an agony beyond anything she had ever felt in her life before.

"I . . I shall be . . all right."

"That is not what I asked you."

There was silence, then he said:

"Answer my question, Romana. Do you want to leave me?"

"I . . want you to be . . happy"

"And you think it will make me happy if you go away?"

"You did not . . want to be married . . and although I tried to leave you . . Mr. Barnham said it would . . harm you because Lord Kirkhampton would make a . . scandal . . but now he is . . dead."

"He is dead," the Marquis agreed, "because you killed him to save me."

"So now . . you are . . free . . as Nicole is."

"As Nicole is," the Marquis repeated. "Shall we talk about Nicole first?"

He did not wait for Romana to reply but said:

"I found Nicole at her house as I expected, resting before the evening's performance. When I told her that Lord Kirkhampton was dead she cried, and they were tears of relief."

Romana drew in her breath, but she did not say anything and the Marquis went on:

"I thanked her for sending you to save my life and she told me how Kirkhampton had tricked her into believing they were married and how desperately ashamed she was of the life she has had to lead with him."

"Nicole has always been good," Romana said, "in . . every way."

"I know that now," the Marquis said, "and I admire her for working as she has done to support her father and mother."

Because she thought there was something in his tone which sounded as if Nicole would not have to work in the future, Romana looked at the Marquis and he saw the question in her eyes.

"Nicole told me of her father's position in France before the Revolution," he said, "but neither he nor she seem to be aware that Bonaparte has invited the members of the *Old Regime* to return to France, and in many cases has restored to them their properties, or at least, some part of what was confiscated during the Revolution."

"Do you mean . ." Romana began.

She was interrupted as the Marquis went on:

"The reason I was away for so long was that I took Nicole to see a friend of mine, the Duc de Graumont who is leaving for Paris within the next few days. He remembered the Comte de Prêt and he will make every enquiry to see what can be done about his position."

"How wonderful if the Comte could get back his estates!"

"My friend the Duc was certain that if not all the estates could be restored to him there would certainly be some money available in compensation for what he has lost."

Romana clasped her hands together.

"Oh, thank you, thank you!" she said. "The Comte and Comtesse have always been so kind to me and it will mean so much to them now they are old and in ill health."

"That is what Nicole said," the Marquis replied, "and when I left her she was very happy. In fact, she has arranged to have supper with the Duc later this evening, so that they can go into the matter further."

Romana felt her heart leap.

At least the Marquis would not be having supper with Nicole if she was with the Duc.

"What is more," the Marquis continued, "I think the Duc before he leaves for France will introduce Nicole to some of the French Colony in London. As her father's daughter she will find a social circle only too willing to receive her, and she will soon have a number of new friends who will be very different in every way from the man who has made her life a misery."

Romana drew a deep breath.

"That is . . wonderful too," she said. "Perhaps it was a . . mistake for Nicole to dance at Covent Garden, but she has no other talents that could make money."

"You can stop worrying about her," the Marquis said. "The Duc is sure there will be some money at any rate, coming from France and his wife, the Duchesse, is going to ensure that Nicole is not lonely or without friends until the Duc returns."

"I am so happy for her!" Romana cried.

"Now suppose we talk about ourselves?" the Marquis suggested.

He saw as he spoke Romana give a little quiver, her eye-lashes flickered and she was suddenly acutely conscious that they were very close and in bed together.

Then it struck her once again that he was free of any obligation to the wife he had never wanted to marry.

Now he would be able to send her to one of his other houses, or else, as she had suggested so often, back to Little Hamble from where she had come.

She looked up at him and she was not aware that there was something desperate in the expression in her eyes.

"What . . do you want to . . say to me?"

"You have still not answered my question," the Marquis said. "Do you really want to leave me, Romana?"

"I . . I want to do . . what you want."

He looked at her for a long moment, then he said:

"Perhaps what I want will make you hate me as you did when we were first married."

"That was . . different."

"Why was it different."

"Because I did not know you then . . and you were all muddled up in my mind with . . Lord Kirkhampton."

"That was certainly enough to make you hate anybody!" the Marquis agreed. "But afterwards?"

"Afterwards . . when you helped me with Papa's poems . . I knew you were very different in every way from what I . . had thought you were."

"In fact I was so different that when you had the chance of being free of me you rode through the night to warn me, then saved me by shooting the man who would have murdured me in cold blood."

Romana drew in her breath.

"I . . I suppose I ought to feel that it was . . wrong and wicked to kill anyone . . but I am glad he is . . dead."

"Are you glad I am alive?"

"Yes, of course, very, very glad!"

She spoke impulsively, and now was conscious that the Marquis had drawn a little nearer still.

"When I was carrying you back on my saddle to the Inn," he said, "I found myself translating some verses of Sophocles we had left unfinished the other night. Do you remember where we stopped?"

"I think . . so," Romana said.

"Then perhaps you will not agree with my translation, and yet I think it fits in with what your father had done before."

"Tell me," Romana said.

The Marquis paused for a moment, then he said:

"I think Deianira said:

> ". . . . . . Only a fool
> *Would try conclusions with the God of Love,*
> *Love has his own way with the gods themselves:*
> *Why not with me?*"

"That is clever of you, very clever!" Romana cried.

"I thought the words were apt," the Marquis remarked, "especially where they concern me."

He saw the surprise in Romana's eyes. Then she asked almost in a whisper:

"Why . . should they particularly . . concern you?"

"Because love has had his way with me," the Marquis answered, "and I think, because once again I am being perceptive, Romana, with you too."

For a moment he felt she did not understand, then as the colour flooded into her face, she made a little inarticulate movement and his arms went round her.

He pulled her close against him and she hid her face against his shoulder.

"I have fallen in love, Romana," the Marquis said. "I thought that was what had happened to me the other night when we were translating from Greek in the manner, we

155

hoped, of your father, and I was sure of it when I saw the expression in your eyes when you came across the field towards me this morning."

He drew her a little closer still as he said:

"I knew that you cared a little for me and the anxiety in your voice told me what you had suffered in thinking you had been too late to save me from Kirkhampton's ambush."

The Marquis's lips were against Romana's forehead as he went on:

"I felt then that I had no wish to die, but to live so that I could be with you, and you must have felt the same or you would not have shot Kirkhampton to prevent him from killing me."

There was silence for a moment, then the Marquis said:

"I want to thank you, Romana, and there is only one way I can do it."

As he spoke he put his fingers under her chin and turned her face up to his.

He looked down at her for a long moment. Then he said very quietly:

"Thank you, my darling, for keeping me alive so that I can tell you how much I love you."

Then his lips were on hers and as Romana trembled against him she knew that this was what she had been longing for, this was what she had feared she had lost.

The pressure of the Marquis's lips on hers was not only a rapture and a joy that was indescribable, but was part of everything that was beautiful and inspirational.

She felt as if he gave her the light of Greece and the glitter and wonder of the gods themselves.

There was in his kiss, the divine radiance she had sensed in her father's poems, which now seemed to be translated into something real and living that drew her very soul from between her lips and made it a part of his.

His kiss was so perfect, so glorious, that when he raised his head to look down at her, she gave a little murmur as if she could not bear him to let her go.

"I love you, my darling!" he said, and his voice was very deep and, she thought, a little unsteady. "Now tell me what you feel for me."

"I love . . you! I love . . you! But I thought now that Lord Kirkhampton was . . dead I should no longer be of any . . use to you, that you would want to be . . rid of me."

"You are my wife," the Marquis answered, "and as my wife I will never lose you. We are together, my precious, as I think the God of Love intended from the very beginning."

"Do you really . . think that?" Romana asked. "I am sure it is true . . but you are so . . magnificent . . so wonderful! I am not . . good enough for . . you."

"That is not true," the Marquis replied, "you have already given me back what I had lost and half-forgotten. Now I know there is so much more: a whole world of wonders, far more important than anything I own already."

"Do you mean it . . do you really . . mean that?" Romana asked.

"I am not going to say yes because I want to convince you," the Marquis said, "and the best way is like this."

His lips were on hers again and he was kissing her fiercely, passionately and more insistently than he had before.

He felt her quiver against him and now he drew her body closer and still closer and his lips moved from her mouth to the softness of her neck, then lower until he found her breasts.

To Romana it was as if Apollo himself poured his light upon her so that the sun enveloped her in a golden haze and the glory from it blinded her eyes and swept through her body like a burning flame.

Then the light became more intense and the fire of it leaped within them both and carried them together into the very heart of the sun. . . .

. . . . .

It was much later that the Marquis kissed Romana's forehead and she stirred against his shoulder.

"What are you thinking?" he asked.

"That . . nothing which has happened is . . really true . . but in some mysterious way we have stepped into one of Papa's poems . . and become part of the . . gods ourselves."

157

"That is what I felt," the Marquis said, "and I think, m
darling, we have found *'the fires of God which flame in th
high hill-forests'*."

Romana gave a little cry of delight.

"That was a line just before the ones you translated!"

"I thought you would remember it," he said. "As it wa
true for me, I want it to be true for you too."

"I did not . . know that love could be so . . wonderful, sc
exciting!" Romana said, "and so absolutely and completely
. . beautiful."

"That is because it is real love," the Marquis said, "the
love the Greeks sought and knew, the love you told, my
lovely darling, I must find."

"And have I . . helped you find it?"

"You know the answer to that," the Marquis said with a
smile, "and this is the truth. I never knew that love could be
so perfect and so completely, absolutely satisfying!"

Romana gave a cry of happiness.

"That is the love I . . wanted you to find . . but I was
afraid you would find it with . . somebody else . . rather
than me."

The Marquis drew her closer as he said:

"Were you jealous of Nicole?"

"H . how did you . . know?"

"I think I know everything about you," he said,
"everything that is important. Your eyes, my little love, are
very expressive whether you are hating or loving me."

"I will never ever . . hate you again."

"Is that a promise?"

"How could I do anything but love you when you are so
wonderful? You are the sort of man I always longed to find
but thought he could only be a dream."

"I am real," the Marquis said, "so real that I was terribly
afraid when I came in here a little while ago that I should
frighten you and you would hate me as you did when we
were first married."

"You . . hated me too."

"That was before we understood about love."

"It was Papa's poems which taught me you were . .
different from what I had . . thought."

158

Romana gave a cry and put out her arms to hold him close.

"Supposing," she said, "supposing the Lord Chief Justice had never come to luncheon? You would never have realised that I was Papa's daughter, and I should never have known how different you are from what I imagined you to be!"

"I still believe that love would have found his way," the Marquis smiled. "We were meant for each other, my darling, since the beginning of time. Looking back now I think when I was at Oxford I was searching for you in my mind."

He kissed her hair before he went on:

"Then I lost my way in the social and sporting world, until by chance, or as had been planned from the very beginning, we were together even though we did not at first appreciate the fact."

"You make it sound very . . exciting," Romana said, "but now I am only so grateful . . so very, very . . grateful that I no longer need be . . afraid of Lord Kirkhampton trying to kill you . . but suppose there are . . other men?"

"I cannot believe the world is full of Kirkhamptons," the Marquis said dryly, "but of one thing you may be quite sure."

"What is that?" Romana asked.

"That no man in the future will want revenge because I have taken some woman from him. The only ones who need be frightened now are the ones who try to take you from me."

"No-one will do that," Romana replied. "I am yours . . completely and absolutely . . I belong to you. I was . . thinking. . ."

She stopped speaking and the Marquis prompted:

"What were you thinking?"

"That when you were . . loving me," Romana answered in a very low voice, "you were like Apollo pouring your golden light over me until we both were . . somehow in the . . heat of the sun itself."

"My sweet, my precious one!" he said. "That is what I want you to think."

"You are godlike . . and divine."

"And that is what you are to me."

She could say no more, for the Marquis was kissing her, kissing her fiercely and demandingly.

She could feel the fire on his lips igniting the fire in her and once again they were both enveloped by the light.

It was the light that came from the gods, and the fire of it flamed fiercely and compellingly within them.

THE END